FUCKERY
BY
LINDA CARABALI

Fuckery by Linda Carabali

Copyright © 2022 Linda Carabali

All rights reserved. No portion of this book may be reproduced in any form.

Cover by Linda Carabali

ISBN 9798806289125

For all those who believed in me

ONE

All flights are cancelled. Every single one, fucking grounded. No doubt it's because of bloody COVID-19.

"Naaaa for real what the fuck am I doing?" I say, into the phone.

"*Mate*, what's wrong?" Mazzy asks.

"All the flights are fucking cancelled, dude. Every single one mate."

"Damn, didn't think it was that deep, but seems it is," Mazzy responds.

I look down at my brown leather satchel bag by my feet. I know I shouldn't do things for money, but I do things for fun. I can never resist having bloody fucking fun. So that's why I'm finding myself possibly committing an act of terrorism.

I really didn't mean to.

I don't think I fully understood what I'd actually gotten myself into.

But now I do. It's just sunken in.

Am I ready to die? Naaa, I don't think so…

Do I want to actually become a murderer…? A terrorist…? Naaaa… not really… yeah there's some real scum on this earth, people would probably say I am… but I'm not Trump level, you get me.

I know it's bad, and kind of fucked up but Coronavirus just saved my life and a bunch of others' too.

BBC News is playing on a screen above me, Boris Johnson's mug is spitting some "business as usual" shit.

I burst out laughing, my loudness climbs the ladder of sounds around me. After a minute my laugh overpowers the wheeled suitcases and various shoes tapping the marble floor.

People start looking at me, but I just laugh harder.

I mean come on, I'm used to being the centre of people's attention.

I'm a red fluff-ball… so of course.

"Hey, Elmo are you listening mate?" Mazzy asks and suddenly my attention comes back to my phone. Somehow during the course of my laughter my phone was no longer attached to my ear but instead was flailing about in the air like a madman about to drown at sea. Well, to be fair, I'm lowkey a bit of a madman… naaa scratch that, highkey a madman.

Anyways… bringing the phone back to my ear I ask, "What did you say again Maz?"

"I said it's off. ISIS just ceased their operations so you're in the clear for now. Go home, get high, relax."

"What am I supposed to do with the bomb then? Keep it as a souvenir?" I ask sarcastically.

"You know what, you might as well mate. You never know when it might come in handy. You know what I'd love to have that thing in my living room. Imagine it as a conversation starter with a Tinder date… it'd *literally* guarantee me a fuck." Mazzy is *actually* crazy.

Of fucking course Mazzy would think that's how you get a fuck, but to be honest it would lowkey make a good souvenir…. not gonna lie. And I guess till I figure out what to do with the bomb it's gotta come back with me anyway so….

"Well, thanks for letting me know mate. Imma head back to the flat now talk to you later man, ciao," I say cutting off the line.

Picking up my satchel, I start to turn around and look at the airport. The place is still packed with people. Some are sat down talking to friends and family, some people shouting down their phones having complete meltdowns.

They're all lost in the life. *Lost in the sauce.*

Corona just swallowed up everything.

RIP Holiday plans, yeah.

Now I've gotta find my way to the fucking underground station and get on the Piccadilly line home. This is gonna be so fucking long.

By the time I get to the station I've already seen three people with masks and damn the looks on people's faces when the guys at the station were saying that all flights are cancelled…

You should've bloody seen the woman coming out of the barriers with her pink suitcase. She fully got her suitcase stuck in the barriers, could really tell it was a real struggle for her to get her shit together for her flight. The look on her face when the TFL guy told her it was true, "You've got to be fucking kidding me!" She said, then she fully dropped to the floor. Exhaustion hit her all at once, or maybe she just levelled up.

Stress level 100.

Shit maybe I'm talking about myself, maybe I've just hit stress level 100.

Not gonna lie, seems kind of possible given the fact I'm carrying a fucking bomb on the Piccadilly line right now.

I could seriously get arrested and go to prison any second but then again I've done a lot of illegal things and I still haven't got one criminal conviction so… I'm doing good. I'm the most unsuspicious red furry monster you'll ever meet.

I'm sitting on the tube and I'm holding my satchel in between my feet, in between my legs. I keep looking around all the kids looking at their mums and dads and all the parents looking at their kids and their grandkids and I'm just there sat with a fucking bomb. Like, I could've killed a whole family tree.

Fuck.

I *could* kill all these people right now. *Damn, the fucking power I hold between my legs.*

Don't want you to think that I'm just some psycho. I don't know, like sometimes I'm doing things in life and I don't even understand what I'm doing.

Then I just stop and look at reality through this little window that appears once in a while like, fucking hell how did I get here? But like, you know sometimes… life just happens you know. What's that saying Beyoncé has? When life gives you lemons you make lemonade.

That's what I'm doing right now though, making lemonade out of a bad situation.

Gangster shit.

That's what you're probably wondering, what kind of bad situation was it that the lemonade is a fucking bomb? Let me be the one to tell you man, the world is fucked.

Don't think you understand how life treats furry little red creatures like me, but you know what… I still got it a lot better than some people. Have you seen the amount of hate pages about Wendy Williams? Like don't get me wrong I understand why they exist, I'm still not even sure if she's a woman or man, mate. Not gonna lie... though I think we do all have to accept she's a woman, she's had a kid and all.

Anyway off topic there, the point is life goes on.

A couple hours later, I decide Mazzy wasn't too crazy after all. The bomb looks great on the coffee table. I've got my butt planted on the sofa and my legs stretched out onto the table.

You know what maybe I should go and try out the Tinder thing? Mazzy was right about the bomb in the living room. So maybe he's right about that...

Lowkey think this isn't gonna work but I wanna see if it actually works. Even if this crashes and burns in my face LOL.

Getting my phone, I open up Tinder. Okay I'm swiping...

Brenda, nah she looks dead.

Maddie, she looks mad. Swipe right.

Oxi, cool name. Blue eyebrows, and she plays bass. Definite swipe, and oh look at that— instant match.

Let's get this stuff started.

Hey, wanna link right now? Might be the last chance you get before Miss Rona gets you... I write.

A couple minutes later, she responds. *Yeah I'm down* and sends me her number.

Not gonna lie, this is a little long and that but who cares, init? It's just a bit of fun, am I right?

I press call and wait a bit.

"Hi, there Oxi," I say.

"Hey Elmo, I know I said I'm down to link. But actually I'm sorta having a thing with mates at my yard you know before the whole world falls apart if you wanna come?" She asks.

It's been a while since I've gone to party, but she doesn't know that, and besides life's always a bit of fun when I'm there. Doesn't matter who it is.

"Course, send me the deets, Oxi. See ya later," I tell her ending the call. Seems I won't be able to test out Mazzy's living room bomb theory tonight, oh well there's plenty of time anyways.

A couple of hours later I found myself sat on a sofa again, only difference is this time Oxi is sat on my lap.

Her mates seem calm too, but who wouldn't be with how zonked out they are right now. I feel like I'm sinking into the sofa material and Oxi's skin is blending with my fur.

Maybe I had one too many brownies.

Weed brownies that is, there's like one left on the tray.

The room's filled with art and posters, and there's an electronic disco ball spinning in the corner of the room. Red, green and blue taking turns to help annihilate our visions. This is super trippy. Not gonna lie.

The music playing on the speakers changed, and I feel Oxi's arse grinding into me slowly. She was going round and round. My dick is getting hard. All the while though she was having a conversation with her roommate across the room. I'm too cunted to even be fucking listening let alone participate.

I want a fuck right now.

"Elmo!" At the sound of my name being shouted over the music I turn to Oxi's roommate, Jezza.

"Yeah, Jezza," I say.

"What's 10 + 9?"

"It's twenty-oneeeeee," I say recalling the meme.

"AYEEEEE," Jezza shouts jumping up from his spot on the sofa across and stepping onto the coffee table. "Drink up!" He shouts and downs the rest of the Glen's vodka.

I grab onto Oxi's hips and lift her up off me, as I get up. I grab the last brownie in the tray and scoff it down. I take a cigarette from the pack on the table. The music changed, Travis Scott's Highest in the Room.

With the beat I bop and shift my body, getting lost in the high. I end up standing next to Jezza on the table.

Smooth transition.

I feel my fuzzies, fuzing. I see the room zooming, Oxi's shifting from the sofa to the window, stretched out and smokey all at once. Blue and orange marbling blurring with her before my eyes. Jezza looks so fucking weird. His eyes are huge, and his face looks like it's disappeared behind them.

Oh wait, hang on. This angle…

When did I get on the ceiling?

Because I'm looking down at Jezza looking up at me from the table. He looks funny though.

Damn. Not again!

You know I'm fucked when I'm walking on walls.

Things are moving mad. Blues are in, smoking around the room. It's so spacey up here. The ceiling is so smooth. I've still got the cigarette and lighter in my hand.

"Oh my God!"

I bring the cigarette to my mouth, hold it with kissy lips (to make sure it doesn't fall) and light it up.

"What the fuck?"

I take a drag.

"This is skits"

Exhale.

"Nice ceiling guys," I sing, smiling.

Oh well, might as well enjoy it init.

TWO

When I came back to life I was at home. On my living room floor. A condom lying next to me, used.

I get up, and my butt hurts. There's cum coming out of it. Fuck. *Did someone fuck me?*

For fuck's sake, my arse hurts like a bitch.

This morning can't get any worse…

I look down at the coffee table, and the bomb's gone…

Shit.

Where the fuck is it?

Fucking spoke too soon didn't I?

I grabbed the glass on the table and chucked it on top of my head.

Wasn't water like I'd hoped though. Smells like Vodka.

Feel myself waking up though. Kinda working. My eyes and head are starting to pay more attention. Definitely, well at least I hope so. Still dunno how I got home. Least that's good, right? I actually *got* home. Still lowkey feel like I'm not fully with it, but that's a new day for you. You get up and move. You breathe, you drink, you smoke, you fuck.

I crank my neck, side to side.

CRACK.

Yeah… needed that.

When I came back to it, I saw Jezza was lying down face planted on the rug. Wait, hang on is that— oh shit. He's lying in puke. For fuck's sake, when the fuck did that happen? There's a loud banging coming from behind me. Some shit must've just fallen somewhere. I turn around. I see Oxi, she's holding my Scooby-doo mug.

"El, you're up?"

"Yeah, what you drinking?"

"Irish coffee mate, do you want some?"

"Yeah gimme some of dat b," I say walking over to her. She hands me the mug and I take a swig. "Didn't realise I had whiskey at yard though."

"You didn't."

"Oh so you went out then? What'd you get?"

"Whiskey, condoms, crisps. Picked up some more weed."

"Do ya know where the bomb is? Swear I left it on the coffee table here before I went to yours."

"No idea mate, don't remember anything to be honest."

Taking another swig from the mug I start glancing around at the state of my living room. There was black, bright blue and red spray paint all over the walls, pictures and even the fucking mirror. Giant scribbles of lines and what I'm assuming are empty spray paint cans on the floor.

Damn what the actual fuck happened last night?

Oh well, at least my living room looks like its actually lived in, init. Don't you just find it so jarring when you're walking into people's yards and the house literally has no feeling, it's just this clinical piece of shit. Might as well be a dentist's office, you get me.

MEAOOOOOW.

What was that? I look around at the direction of the sound, it was coming from under the desk in the corner by the window. I walk over and crouch down to find a small little furry kitty.

There's a cat… in my flat….? It looked up at me. Big cute green eyes.

Meow.

"Damn kitty kat, you cute piece of shit. I dunno how you got here but you can stay if you wanna."

I feel Oxi come up behind me, "You've got a cat? Cute."

"Well I do now," I say. Taking the last swig of the mug. Just what I needed to wake up, Irish coffee. Now for a blem.

I reach for my rolling stuff from the desk and walk back to sofa. I start rolling, as I'm licking the paper I look up over at Oxi stroking the cat. I pat myself down, looking for my lighter and realise I'm not actually wearing any jeans. O yeah forgot. Hope the sofa is drying up whoever's cum was coming outta my arse. O but there's a box of matches on the table. Grab that.

Blem between my lips. Furry paws fiddling, got a match out, close the box. Spark it on the side. Light the blem. That first inhale was all I needed. Feels like a good morning. Damn don't even know what fucking time it is. Imma just say morning, I hope it's the morning.

It's not everyday lose track of time.

Actually it kinda is, but I gotta lie to myself like this. To keep myself sane in this madness. You get me.

Taking another drag, I look at Oxi's legs. They were nice legs. Long and inviting. Her mini skirt was the shortest I've seen in a while. Oxi starts shuffling down closer to the cat, her head is eye level to the desk. That bend in her knees.

Blem to lips.

Her ringed hands stop stroking the cat and they reach up under her denim skirt. Delicate fingers hook underneath the sides of her thong and pull them down nice and slowly.

Another drag of my blem.

She starts shimming out of her thong, it falls to the floor and she places her hands on her arse. Then smacks it.

Inhale.

The redness starts exploding on her arse. Then she bends down further. Her cunt now in full view. It's waiting and glistening, impatiently.

Exhale.

I chuck the finished blem in the ashtray, stand up and walk over to her cunt. I grab her sides and dip my head down, running my nose over her juice. She moans. I kneel down for breakfast. I lick and suck like it's fresh fruit. But to honest it smells more like fruit that's gone off. But we move init. That's just life. Pussy doesn't smell like Marc Jacobs. Pussy smells like sex. Like wanton desire for pleasure. Pussy smells like a good time. Oxi's wetness tastes like a good time.

This is gonna be a good morning.

Her cunt buzzing like a follow request beneath me. I accept, slipping my tongue inside. She moans again.

My dick moves.

She's grinding on my mouth.

My dick stands.

She's moving her legs further apart. My hands come up to her sides, and I pull myself up. I tower above her bent body. I insert my furry red dick and start to fuck her. As my fur became completely drenched, my dick gets slicker. The penetration gets faster, the bitch gets louder.

The desk shakes the wall with every moan. The cat sprints out before it got squished to death like a pancake. I keep fucking the cunt.

I hear scuffling behind me.

Moan.

"OUCH! WHAT THE FUCK!" Jezza's just woken up I hear. I look the back to where he was lying before, there's two giant red lines across his forehead. Yikes, that looks bad. He's looking at the cat, and the cat's looking down at him innocently.

"Shit— Jezza— cat got you— good," Oxi says.

"No shit Sherlock," he says sitting up.

I turn my head to look at Oxi's back again. Her head's turning back too, her eyes catch mine. Her big brown ones, her mouth gapes as I'm fucking her. Blem would be good right about now. Can't deal with them eyes. They look emotive. Wish I could look at her tits, but bitch kept them clothed.

"Jezza, roll me a blem mate. Stuff's on the sofa."

Moan.

"Sure, mate."

I look up at the spray painted mirror, and watch Jezza move himself to the sofa. He starts rolling. The cat walks past him. I follow the cat with my eyes, it sits by the door.

I'm still fucking the cunt. She's probably had her fill. When am I gonna cum? For fucks sake, where's that blem?

The cat's still sitting there by the door.

"Jezza, where's that blem?"

Moan.

"Here," Jezza says. I turn my head, and he's already by us. I grab the blem from him and he hands me a lighter from his pocket. I light the blem and smoke. My eyes close, and my hips move slower.

Another fucking moan from Oxi, makes me look down at her. She's looking at me. I blow smoke in her face and I finally fucking cum.

I pull out and white semen spatters outta the cunt.

I take another drag. Oxi has the potential to be a good fuck, but today wasn't it. *That* wasn't it, couldn't wait for that shit to be over. Fucking on a Monday is always shit.

"Oi, I didn't cum. Don't stop."

"I did."

"I haven't."

"Bitch, I'm soft."

"Fuck you."

"Just did."

She looks at me like she's about to cry, like I'm supposed to feel sorry for her. I just met her yesterday. "Mate just finish her off," Jezza says.

He cares… or maybe he's just nice. I don't remember much of last night but since he just rolled me a blem while I fucked his mate…

Eh… Yeah I decide. Jezza's nice.

I take another drag from my blem. "For fuck's sake," I say and insert my fingers.

She moans.

I fuck her cunt faster. She moans louder.

I add another finger, she starts screaming. DRAMATIC much, but I keep moving. She's nearly done.

BANG.

Moan.

BANG, BANG.

Louder moan.

BANG!

Screams.

The door bursts open.

Guys in black helmets and uniforms filter into the living room with guns.

I'm still finger fucking the cunt. I take the last drag from my blem and chuck it on the floor.

Oxi screams for the last time, and she cums.

Another random guy in a suit comes into the flat and walks over to me. He pulls my wrist out of the cunt, and pulls it behind me. He pulls my other one next to it and slaps some metal cuffs on my wrists.

Am I getting arrested?

"Elmo you are being arrested for suspicion of commission, preparation and instigation of terrorist acts. You have the right to remain silent. Anything you say can and will be used against you in a court of law. You have the right to an attorney. If you cannot afford an attorney, one will be provided for you."

I've just gotten arrested.

Good fucking morning, my arse. I wanted to suck her cum off my fingers though. What's the point in all that hand exercise if I don't get to relive the okay oral before this shit fuck?

My hands are cuffed behind my back tightly.

I won't licking no pussy no more.

Fuck.

THREE

This day just keeps getting better and better. Why am I in a police interrogation room? Might have something to do with terrorism and the bomb.

Yeah, that's probably it.

This day got so long so quick. One minute I was enjoying my blem, having okay sex and the next I'm at some police station. The arrest was a bit mental, well for Jezza and Oxi. I didn't really care, or resist.

But those two they resisted alright. Jezza opened the window in the living room but while he was debating whether or not he'd survive the jump those guys in black got him. They pushed him to the ground, and slapped cuffs on him. With Oxi she tried to pull her thongs back up her arse but didn't get the chance to. Pretty sure she's in an interrogation room like me right now with no underwear. Damn, I don't envy her. Imagine the cold slab of the metal and having your cunt right on it, naked. Not the one and I'm pretty sure my cum is still up in there. Yikes. Wouldn't wanna be the cop that has to clean that chair after she gets up.

"How long have you wanted to kill hundreds of innocent lives?" Dyer says. He's the guy who pulled my hand out of Oxi's cunt.

"I haven't *actually* wanted to."

"Oh, really now?" Dyer says. "I've got reason to believe you were about to set a bomb off at Heathrow Airport yesterday."

"Well, I wasn't."

"We have multiple witnesses to place you at the scene. We even have you on CCTV. Don't lie to me, Elmo. It won't get you anywhere." He says. I grimace.

"Your friends have told us you had a bomb. They've given you up. Might as well save your own skin right now. Or else you'll be going away for a very long time." Mazzy would never give me up.

"What friends you talking about here?" I ask.

"Mr. Jezza Scott and Miss Oxi Moron."

Relief.

Those two, eh they were fun. Too bad I can't remember what fucking happened the most of last night. "I literally met them yesterday," I say. Still think it would've been better to fuck Oxi somewhere hot, like Spain.

Damn, am I ever gonna see the outside again? Let alone another fucking country.

"Regardless, point still stands. We know you have the bomb. Where is it? We searched your flat. It's not there. Miss Moron seems to be under the impression it's in your flat."

"I don't fucking know. If it's not in my flat somewhere then I really dunno where it is."

Damn. That bitch was the last person I fucked. It wasn't great but I already miss it.

Sex.

"So you agree to the existence of said bomb?" Dyer smirks. "Where did you learn to make that? Looked at your file— you haven't been in the army, special ops… so where exactly did you learn?"

"Look, here Dyer," I say, "Does it look like I know how to make a bloody fucking bomb? What do you think this is? This ain't a fantasy drama, or lala cuco-land. It's the real world. Reality. Why'd you think I'd waste my time learning to do shit like that. It ain't fun. Fucking cooking ain't fun, mate."

This guy is actually fucking stupid. Why would I, a perfect furry red monster waste my time on that skill. There's better things in life to spend your time on. Smoking, drinking, fucking...

Bet he doesn't get much.

"I'm not your mate. Then if you didn't make it — who did?"

Yep. He's got a stick up his arse. Oh shit. I nearly forgot about the fact cum was coming outta my arse this morning. Really wish I could remember who did me, then I wouldn't have this morning's shit fuck as a last reminder of my now ever-distant sex life.

Maybe Dyer can tell me. Seems like a stalker, he's got nothing else to do. "If you know so much about me, then you tell me," I say.

"You don't know do you?"

Silence.

"Who gave this bomb to you?"

Silence. When's this guy gonna shut up?

"Why were you at Heathrow Airport yesterday?" He slides a picture of me looking at the cancelled flights while on the phone onto the table.

Silence.

"If you don't talk I can't help you."

"What can you do for me? You've arrested me because you think I'm a terrorist. Don't think I'll be able to have a normal life again anyways, after this."

"You're calling your life normal? That's rich given your history. Your record is littered with misdemeanours. You've been living life on a tight rope, Elmo."

"Well, I like to have fun."

"You're a sicko. You think being a terrorist is fun?"

"I'm not a terrorist."

"I'm losing my patience here, Elmo."

"I'm losing my will here, *mate,*" I say. Dyer's hands clench on the table. He looks pissed. Serves him right. Twat.

"Your will to be a terrorist, yes. That's good."

"No, my will to live," I say, correcting him. "You lot are gonna lock me up and throw away the key. Even if you don't find anything. I'd honestly rather die. What's the point of being locked up in a four by four foot square room with nothing?"

Ah. Damn. I'm thirsty right now. How long have I been here?

Fuck.

"I *can't* fuck, drink, smoke…"

Could really do with a blem right about now and a wank. What I'd do to have a good pair of tits pressed up against my back right now. A hot cunt on my dick right now, sliding up and down.

My dick…

I reach for my cock, the cuffs rattling on the table as I try to move them to my lap. My paws get stopped. RIP to my wank.

"What do you think you're doing Elmo?" Dyer asks. "KEEP YOUR HANDS ON THE TABLE."

Ooouh Dyer got feisty. Me likey.

My dick just twitched.

"I'm tryna have a wank, mate."

"You what?"

"Wank. You know, jerk off. Masturabtion, you ever tried it?" I ask. He looks so pissed right now. So, so done. The more he gets pissed off, the harder my dick gets.

Bet he wishes I hadn't chosen to represent myself in here. If I had an attorney they would've straight up told me to say no comment to everything. I've watched the films. My soul would have no fun that way though, for sure.

Or my dick.

"*You…*"

I can feel my fur getting wet. *The pre-cum's started.*

"Aaaa, come on. Lighten up. It's just me, mate. Come on, help me out. Jerk me off, I don't care just need a release, you get me. This shit's painful. Like I had a shit fuck this morning, just not my day. A furry monster's got needs mate. So you gonna help me or not? Oh and mind getting me a blem while you're at it."

If he doesn't believe me, all he has to do is look under the table. He'll find my red stallion standing nice and strong.

"You've got to be fucking kidding me. You… *you're acting like this*. DISGUSTING! You sound worse than my teenage son. I lost my libido a long time ago, so unfortunately I don't know how you feel right now nor do I care to be frank. But what I can offer you is a deal."

"A deal?"

"You become our informant. You tell us everything we want to know. We own you. You won't be locked up, but you'll be on a tight leash."

"So you want me to become a snitch?"

"I want you to be my bitch."

Snitches end up in ditches. I've been around long enough to know that.

"Can I have a blem to think about it?" I ask. He looks at me long and hard, then takes out a straight. He leans over the table. Puts it in my mouth and then lights it.

"You've got five minutes, after that— offers up. Then… I don't know what will happen to you. If I were you I'd take the deal."

I take a drag.

"Don't be stupid, Elmo." He says, standing up from his seat. The chair's legs screeched on the floor, and he walks out the door. It slams shut.

Exhale.

I'm just more surprised they're letting me smoke inside a police station.

I don't exactly know why they got onto my scent. Doesn't seem like he *actually* knows anything. If he did, he would've come at me with more aggression. I mean if he knew about Mazzy and ISIS. Seems he doesn't. Deal wouldn't be on the table though that's for sure. I'd probably be dealt with by bigger, shadier big cheeses.

For all he knows… the bomb could've been fake. Faulty.

I don't really get it. Don't really care. I'm going to accept this deal.

Can't wait to have a fuck after this. Wonder if there's anyone in this police station that's a *little* bit of me?

FOUR

Life's about fun, you get me. It's not about taking shit seriously, you try do that and you're not gonna be ready to die, ever.

I die everyday. I make it a daily goal. Some people have a step count, I have a death count. I'm laughing, I die and come back to life so many fucking times. No matter what happens, shit just doesn't faze me. Imagine being bothered by random shit that don't matter, on a daily. What a fucking drag.

Dyer let me go, but not before chatting utter shit to me for fucking ages. Complete waste of my bloody time. I could've been home with a beer and a body, but NOOOO.

Apparently, Jezza and Oxi were released as well. Turns out Oxi got a warning or something because of the weed she'd picked up that morning.

Eventually, I did reach home. If I thought when I'd woken up that morning that my flat looked like shit with Jezza's face planted on the floor in vomit, Oxi doing whatever, a fucking cat just chilling there and my living room spray painted to fuck. Well, I want that back.

My living room now, looks unliveable. Everything is trashed. The coffee table is the only thing left standing. The desk is destroyed, looks like they took a hammer to it or some shit. Everything that was on my shelves has been thrown on the floor, and even… *the sofa.* Looks like they took knives and tried to gut it for the butcher shop.

I walk into my kitchen, trashed.

My bedroom is also trashed.

At least they didn't murder the bathroom. Otherwise where would I take a shit?

My phone starts ringing. Damn, where the hell is it though? I haven't seen that thing in a while. Quickly pacing back to the living room I find it lying in the sofa's stuffing. Caller ID says it's Mazzy. I pick up.

"What the fuck Elmo, I've been trying to get a hold of you for fucking ages. Where have you been?" Mazzy asks.

"Police station. Got arrested."

"Arrested? For what?"

"They thought I was a terror—" The line cuts off. Fuck's sake, he could've at least let me finish my fucking sentence. Well, to be fair I understand his paranoia but still…

Need a drink.

Definitely out of alcohol, gotta go shop. Need to roll myself a blem too, but first coffee. I go to the kitchen and use up the last of my coffee. Extra strong, extra dark, the smell is perfect. I take my coffee to the living room and sit on the fucked sofa.

Damn, though.

Sofa's seen some pain but at least it probably felt good. Rough, and torturous. Like it was never going to end. Pain hits you in fazes and makes you think it'll go on forever in that moment. Your head is a liar. After the moment's gone, you'll miss it, and come to love the pain. Regardless of its many forms.

That's why I love dying. Every time I resurrect I live better.

When I was sitting down I accidentally spilled some coffee, it hit my leg. *Ouch.* I watch as it sinks into my red fur. Coffee spillage, helloooo stain. Imma need a shower soon.

When's the last time I showered?

Take another swig from my mug. Spilled some more, this time it hits the sofa's white stuffing.

Damn, that coffee stain isn't gonna come outta there. I'm not gonna wash it. Can't be bothered. Unless cum can wash it off? Who knows what might happen… eh—let's let the world decide, huh?

Putting my coffee on the table, I look around the floor for the rolling shit. Grab it off the floor, roll myself a blem and smoke.

I need to get up. I have to go to the shops for essentials.

But first I gotta get my shit together.

While smoking my blem, I look around for my shit. I find a pair of dutty jeans and put them on. Grab my keys and wallet and I'm outta the door.

I try to lock it shut but there's no point.

I leave my flat unlocked. It's trash anyway, no one's gonna steal anything. There's nothing to fucking take anyway.

The police really fucked that door. Need to get a handyman. Fucking long. Imma ask Dyer if they can replace that, *they broke it*.

When I get to the shop I buy 3 bottles of red wine, 4 bottles of Cherry B, 3 bottles of Glen's vodka and more tobacco.

As I'm walking out I see a dog tied to the newsstand of the corner-shop. It starts growling at me.

I give it the middle finger and walk to the park. After sitting on a bench and I roll another blem.

A woman runs past me, she looks sweaty and sticky.

I open a bottle of wine and down half of it.

She stops and bends over to tie her shoelace. Her arse looks good in those leggings. I take another swig and smoke a bit more. I'd fuck her. Yes, definitely, my dick thinks so too.

He's active.

She starts doing lunges, and I down the rest of the bottle.

She's active.

I gather my shit into the bag and approach her. "Yo b, what you saying?"

"What?" She asks. She doesn't understand.

"You think I'm cute?" I try. She gives me twinkly eyes. That was easy. Evening snack sorted. Mc Donald's can piss off.

"Of course, you're red and fluffy." Women are so stupid, and too much effort. She's now turned around fully to face me, and reached her hand out to my arm. She strokes my fur.

With one paw I grab her by the jaw. I bring my mouth to hers. The kiss was mild, the wine in me stronger. My other paw came to her back pushing her up against me. I could feel the swell of her breasts on my fur. I wanted her naked.

It was already getting dark in the park. I didn't realise the day had really come and gone.

She kisses me harder, fisting my reds. She must be losing herself in my softness. I drop the blue bag holding my shopping.

I want to feel her smooth skin, I want to feel that human rawness I lack.

"I wanna fuck you," I tell her.

"Let's go," she says. She starts walking off ahead of me. I quickly pick up my shopping bag. As I'm following her I opened a Cherry B bottle with my lighter, downed that in one gulp. Then repeated with another.

She opens the gate to the children's park. There are no children here. It's the night.

We'll be the only children here tonight.

She walks around the various climbing frames and swings. I get in the sandpit, sit and roll a blem.

She's topless on the swing.

Another Cherry B downed and I sink into the sand.

She's started to swing back and forth. Her tits are jumping, her hair flows with the wind.

Inhale.

She walks over to the sandpit, kicks off her trainers and peels off her leggings. I look at the curve of her body. She's trained it well. She's got fat tits, I want to grab them.

Exhale.

She steps down into the sandpit and lays down. She starts to move her legs and dig herself down under. Her body is under the sand, and her torso is raised propped up by her arms. Her tits are hanging down, swinging slowly with her soft movements. Her eyes looked black. She's crawling towards me. Sand is spitting out from her sides.

Inhale.

I open my legs out wide, her elbows drag her into my cone. I look down at her, all I can see is the white line parting the curtains draping down her face. Her head comes down on my dick.

Exhale.

Her wet mouth is slathering me as another Cherry B slaters my throat. Her head keeps bobbing up and down, and all around. I'm struggling to keep my balance in the sand. She starts sucking and I start screaming. When I cum she lifts herself up, my cream smeared all over her mouth. Sand granules stick around her chin and neck.

I lost my blem.

She walks over to my blue shopping bag and takes out the vodka and a lighter. Bitch opens the cap, raises it above her head and pours all of it on herself like a shower. She laughs looking down at me and chucks the bottle behind her.

She takes another vodka out of the bag.

Coming over, she plants a leg by each of my sides, then pours the bottle all over me.

My body is drenched.

Chucking the bottle behind her, she pushes my fat belly down with her foot. Bitch sinks herself onto my red furry dick.

She sparks the lighter and brings it to her breast. She bursts into blue flames, from her breast down to her cunt. Her blue flames used my slick vodka dick as a bridge to my body.

I lay back into the sand as the flames engulf my liquor drenched body, I'm drunk on her cunt. This animal on top of me still bouncing up and down. Rough and hard. Sand is flying everywhere. I can start feel to it sticking to my back.

This shit is gonna be HELL to wash off.

I start to wonder why I wanted to fuck her in the first place…

Ah, yes…

Her tits, I look at them. Pale breasts alight with blue flames. Grabbing onto them tightly I use them to pull myself out from under the sand.

Well, she has been training her body so, someone has to put those abs into good use.

I was sinking.

She screams.

Her cunt feels tighter.

I called this bitch a woman. She's more like a beast.

Life's a joker, I don't think I was in mood to domesticate another bitch tonight.

I'm tired.

Devil is bouncing on my dick, she's moaning. I'm squirming.

She is the monster I should be. I'm screaming.

She laughs. I cum yet she keeps going. This is painful. I can feel myself going limp, yet devil's still fucking me. I grunt and devil smilies. She's playing. There's sand stuck to her rack but…

I'm the bitch.

Fun.

I'm tired of chasing it, the devil just killed me.

Life's the fucking same, you'll watch me die again.

FIVE

I've been in the bath for an hour now.

You don't understand how long it took to get all that fucking sand outta my fur. Like for real, the amount of shampoo I went through… I'm all out now. I've been sitting here soaking in conditioner, gotta keep that fur fluffy.

Looking at all the little bits of sand floating around me is disgusting. I open the tap for more hot water, maybe the granules will float away from me. It doesn't work.

Ooo it's hot.

Damn, it's too hot.

Feels like I'm about to boil. A shiver runs down my spine as I remember that devil. Pain.

I want a blem so bad right now. It's time I get out. My fur is completely soaked, this will take ages to dry off, dammit. At least I no longer smell like vodka. That crazy fucking bitch. When I get to the living room I sit down on the (still) ruined sofa.

Something is poking into my arse.

I shift to the side, and see a small black brick phone. When the fuck did that turn up? Pretty sure that wasn't there before I went out to get essentials.

Well, to be fair anyone could've come in while I was gone. The door was unlocked. As we all know that wasn't my fault. It's the fucking police's.

Before I inspect this trap phone, I'm gonna roll a blem. As I'm about to spark the phone starts ringing.

I pick up, "Hello? Who dis?"

"Elmo, it's me," Mazzy says. I start my blem.

"Oh hey Maz, what's up?" I ask while opening a leftover bottle of wine from *that* demonic fuck.

"What do you mean '*whats up'?* You fucker," he says. He sounds like he's pissed. Oh shit, maybe he knows...

Act calm, normal. I take a swig from the bottle.

"Damn what got your panties in a twist mate, calm down."

"CALM DOWN?" He screams. That didn't work. Shit.

Inhale.

"Yeah, mate. Take a chill pill."

"You motherfucker," he says.

Exhale.

At least it sounds like he's lowkey calmed down though.

"Ah come on now, let's not insult me. Only I insult me," I say with a laugh. Come on laugh back. Let's lighten the mood.

"You know what happens to snitches." Another drag. My laughter definitely fell on deaf ears. I'm screwed.

Bottle to lips. Swig.

"You know about that?" I ask.

"Who do you take me for?"

"Well, you didn't know I'd gotten arrested so I figured you wouldn't know," I say.

"Wow."

"They didn't know about you though, or anything important really, but the bomb," I say. He stays silent for a while so I roll another blem.

"Bullshit."

"Naaaa, for real," I say.

"Then how'd they find out?" He asks.

"Not sure to be honest," I say and light the second blem. "Like they knew I had a bomb but had no idea about anything else."

"And they let you go so you'd lead them to the bigger fish?" He asks.

"Yeah, pretty much," I say and take another drag.

"Hmm…" He starts, "It's a good thing then that I put this trap phone in your yard then. By the way, they really tipped your place upside down man."

"Yeah, I know." I say looking around, I grimace at the cat killing a rat in the corner. I better not find more dead rats hidden in yard like little surprises.

Maybe I should get the cat some food? Maybe it'll stop eating rats.

"But I love the spray paint dude, suits your yard," Maz says.

"Yeeeee, thanks Maz…." I say. Damn though, I completely forgot about that. Thank fuck I don't have to see Oxi and Jezza again. Look at the trash that's made love to my life. Ever since I met those two motherfuckers. Naaaa…

"Where'd you hide the bomb in the end? My living room suggestion was crap init." He obviously doesn't know I actually thought his idea was THE SHIT. Only thing is… I dunno where it's gone.

"Where'd I hide it…?" I laugh shakily. Damn nerves, I'll smoke them away; I take a drag.

Exhale.

"Elmo… don't tell me… you don't have—"

"NO, NO, NO!" I shout.

"Then where is it?"

"It's in a safe place. Thats all you need to know," I say. I hope he buys it.

Dear Fuck Gods,
Please receive this holy libation.
Let my good low-key, high-key terrorist friend buy my bullshit.
Amen.

I pour the rest of the wine bottle onto the rug. There, hopefully that libation should work.

1, 2, 3…

"Well, they've got a job for you," Maz says. He brought it. Thank *fuck* for that.

"But I did the last one, it's not my fault Coronavirus got in the way," I say.

"*Not my problem mate*, they haven't written off your debt."

"What do they want now?" I ask. This could be bad, really bad. Do I want to get in over my head again…? Actually, yeah, life's more fun this way, "But this better be it. Like this one thing and I'm done. Finished, finito? Comprende?"

"I'll try, O.K, but no promises," he says. That's the best I'll ever get. I'll take that.

"This will for sure be a step in the right direction though, you know they wanted to kill you right there and then when people heard you'd turned into a rat. I put my neck on the line for you. Don't let me down."

"You didn't have to do that," I say.

"You'd be dead right now," he says.

"When am I not?" I laugh.

"For fuck's sake, be serious here; this isn't the time for your bullshit." He's got a point.

This is real life shit.

"AYEEEE, yeah, baby."

"*Elmo…*"

"OKAAAAY, jeeze. What do they want me to do?"

"Go to BoJo's yard and leave the bomb there," he says.

"BoJo?" I ask.

"Boris Johnson," he replies. They want me to assassinate the Prime Minister, *I'm soooo down.*

"SIGN ME THE HELL UP," I scream. Maz laughs. "ISIS tryna rid the world of that zip-liner twat. I soooo stan."

"Yeah for real, if you'd used up that bomb in the original plan, would've been a waste," he says.

"Yeah…"

"Anyways, with Corona and shit, he's taking reporters at his house in a while. I'll send you the deets."

"Safe, Maz."

"Good luck." Yeppp I'm going to need it.

I gotta find out what happened to that bomb. *Shit.*

SIX

You know what I need right now? I need a blem, alcohol and a fuck. I go to the kitchen and take a beer. I put Mazzy's trap phone in the bread box tin and take out my normal phone.

Let's open up Tinder. Need new specimens.

Yash, nope he looks boring.

Chloe, she looks like hard work. Swipe left.

Katie, she looks okay. Swipe right.

Apollo, nice name; love the Greeks. He looks like a twat but his bio says *if you're a Tory swipe left.* Okay then, I swipe right.

Mary, another bore. Swipe left. As I waste time swiping for the next twenty minutes, Apollo matches with me and messages me, *Elmo I had to match with you the moment I saw you, I have a favour to ask.*

This random dude doesn't even know me and already wants something from me? Well, who am I to judge, everyone on this app wants something. It's not like I'm *not* looking for quick fucks, you get me.

What's dis favour you want? I type back, as I wait for a response I finish the beer in my hand and roll a blem.

I want you to work for me, he responds.

Work for you as what? I write.

A mascot, for some pictures. A one-time thing, your look is just what I'm looking for. I stare at the message. He can't be serious can he? Well, maybe he is… But this is Tinder so… But then again like… I'm serious when I say I want a fuck, you get me.

I don't mind but it wont't be free, I write.

What do you want? He asks.

I'd probably want you to be my bitch. I take another drag of my blem.

That can be arranged. I smirk at my screen.

Text me, I write and add my number.

I walk back into the living room and stretch out onto the fucked up sofa. I'm smoking my blem and texting Apollo about meeting up. Seems he's keen to meet today and I have nothing to do. It's about 3AM right now and I've agreed to meet him at midday. I think I might hit the sack tonight. It's been a while since I've got some shut eye, not gonna lie.

I'm not sure what time it is when I wake up, but I can say it's definitely morning. The sun's out and it's bright. Every time the light sits on my face, my eyes feel like they're burning.

I feel asleep on that nasty sofa, but least the cat kept me company. Kinda like having this little kitty kat.

When I look at my phone I see three missed calls, Apollo. Seems I've overslept. Oh well, he's the one that wants a favour. He'll wait.

Thirty minutes later I'm waiting at the station for Apollo. When I see him approach me, he waves. "Hey, sorry I'm late. Came from the office."

"Not that deep," I say.

"Although it's way past midday, isn't it Elmo? If you knew you'd be late you should've told me. I waited for you here for like nearly forty-five minutes."

"I get that, I do, but I overslept."

"O.K. What's with the bag?" He asks, referring to my Sainsbury's bag for life.

"Just some stuff for later, init."

"I don't get it but okay, let's go. The favour's waiting for you," he says.

We were at a Labour campaign meeting. Apollo dressed me up, placed a Labour sign attached on some string around my neck and it hung down covering my belly. We took lots of pictures with different people I'd never even heard of.

Last person I heard of to do with Labour was Jeremy Corbyn, pretty sure they were meeting today about selecting a new candidate. Not really sure why he wanted me, but when I saw the Labour colour I kinda understood.

Red.

And of course, I'm a big red furry monster. I attract attention. People come to me, that's just me, init.

Apollo said that the pictures would end up on Labour's socials.

"The fucking conservatives have ruined this country," he says. I nod. "They don't even care about the people. Just look at the bloody world; China's put everyone on lockdown, Spain too, USA's got a travel ban, France's closed everywhere that isn't essential, Italy's on lockdown and the UK… right I know what to do I'll put the kettle on. For fuck's sake."

"Yeah I know right," I say. Then I down the rest of my beer.

After we'd finished Apollo's little advertisement photoshoot for Labour, I'd suggested we go into the Weatherspoons across the street. It was a weekday, but it was packed. We barely managed to find a table. I guess people are scared pubs are going to disappear… But with Tories in government we have nothing to worry about just yet.

We can all still get our fill.

We can all keep on living.

Business as usual.

"Like I— of course, lockdown would be crazy, it's hard the fathom that life would just have to come to a halt like that but… being in lockdown for 3 weeks or more with my family *will* end up with at the least one of us dead and *not* from the virus."

"Oh, if I had to be in lockdown with my family I'd probably go out looking to get contaminated, go back home and cough on all of them. Not gonna lie," I say.

Apollo laughs, "Be like— piss me off and I'll cough."

"Init, or like, gimme the toilet paper or I'll cough," I say. "Man I wish though, I live alone."

"Still though either way, we should be in lockdown but Boris is like 'many more families are going to lose loved ones before their time,'" he says. "Oh so, just wash your hands for twenty-seconds, bloody bullshit."

"He's basically Lord Farquaad from Shrek— some of you… MAY DIE but… it's a *sacrifice* I am willing to make," I laugh.

"Basically just telling the UK he doesn't give a flying fuck and they should just go die," he says.

"Putting it simply, yeah, Boris is a twat."

I really need to find that bomb for the next time Mazzy calls me, then that twat will be gone. Good riddance, the world would be a safer place.

I bet Apollo would be happy to see that bloody bastard Boris dead.

"You don't have to tell me," he says.

"I can see that. You got me to help out with the Labour stuff. Now for my payment," I say. "Follow me."

I get up from the booth we were sitting at, and move towards the end of the pub. I push open the door to the bathroom and go into an empty toilet cubicle. Apollo shuffles in after me and I lock the door.

Apollo seems to understand what I want. He unbuckles his belt, and his trousers fall to the floor.

"Doing it in a Wetherspoons loo, always a first," he says. His white briefs don't do much for him, he's tiny. I push him to the white titled wall with my body, and smack my paw around his neck.

He shoves down his boxers, and loosens himself up with his fingers. He gasps soundlessly while he stretches himself.

The sight of his pale face flushed red turns me on. My dick gets hard. I take it in my paw and rub it a bit, feel it grow. I take my other paw off Apollo and pump the rest of my cock with it.

Apollo bends over the toilet seat. Arse upwards giving me full view of his cunt, limp dick and ball sac dangling downwards with gravity. His hands grip the tank as he braces for impact. My paws grab his love handles and in one movement I shove my furry red dick in.

He bites his shoulder.

I push in further, this is getting harder. My dick's stuck. At times like these I miss the devil's vodka sand-soaking ritual. The fuck was smooth. This is gonna take effort.

Oh well, I asked for it. Can't stop before it's even begun. I just had a beer. Need this fuck, then possibly a blem, naaaa scratch that, defo a need a blem after this.

I plunge in further, my hips start thrusting, slowly.

Moan.

Bitch is losing his composure.

In.

Hands grab either sides on the toilet seat.

Out.

"AHHHH!" He screams and I plow into him again. Blood starts spilling down his thighs. Whatever teared up there, just made my dick slicker. Thank fuck.

I penetrate faster.

"AHHHH!"

He falls faster. Bitch's head is two-seconds from falling into the toilet bowl, his forehead bashing into the tank is the only thing saving him from further shame.

Looks like experience though. People probably played dunking donuts with this bitch, must've been fun.

I need to hurry this up, he's making so much noise someone's bound to come in.

Another scream.

His cunt is clamping, is he about to take a shit right now? He better not.

PISSSSSSSSSSS.

I keep fucking him as his pee drips onto my feet. I grab his dick and aim it at the toilet bowl. I keep thrusting, it soaks his face.

DRIP, DROP, BLUP.

It pools into his open mouth. Bitch is drowning in his own piss. It's his fault, he's overflowing…

He looks so small, so weak and disgusting. I laugh.

He starts to choke.

"You're my bitch," I grunt.

"I'm— your— b…itch," he moans.

I shoot him.

Bitch screams.

I pull out, the cum spatters. White and red streaming down his legs. I lift my paw from his side, and clamp it down on the back of his neck. "Don't forget to pay for my drink, bitch."

I shove his head into he toilet bowl.

SPLASSSSH.

His knees BANG to the floor.

I move towards the door and look back, he hasn't moved. "Pathetic," I say and leave.

Well, that was fun.

That's what life's about, you get me.

SEVEN

I'm waiting for the kettle to boil when the phone rings. A number I don't recognise. I answer anyways.

"Elmo?" It's Jezza.

"How did you get my number?"

"Got it off Oxi, mate," he says.

"What do *you* want?" I ask.

"It's about what happened with the police, init. Just wanted to say I'm sorry I kinda dropped you in shit you know…"

"Fuck off."

Silence.

"Is that it…?" I ask.

Silence.

"O.K. Bye," I say and cut the line.

It's nearly about 5 PM since I got back from Spoons. To say the least, I won't be fucking Apollo again. Lemme delete his contact details. There, pussyo's gone.

There's a lot of people you just sort of fuck and never see again. That's just life but it's fun. You never really know what you're getting. Sometimes you do though, because people are stupid and I have eyes, you get me. Read vibes. Apollo, the total wet-wipe versus the devil from the park last night. Damn, what a difference.

Innocent jogger went to devil in the sandpit.

Sex.

Brings out different selves, you get me.

Sometimes, I slyly like being a bitch. But I never know till I'm in the moment. It's like a high.

Every time I think back to earlier today I keep breaking into laughter, Apollo man. That twat, name really doesn't suit him. Named after the Greek God of sun, music, poetry and prophecy, son of Zeus, King of the Gods.

More like Apollo, God of piss.

I'm in the mood for warmth. Once in a while, that's just as fun… but I have to play nice or it'll fuck up…

Again.

I scroll down and call her. It's been long enough. She should've cooled down since then. She picks up.

"Doja, how's you?" I ask.

"Good, you?"

"Oh, you know me. I'm always alright b," I say. I can hear her smile.

"Why'd you call?"

"Oh… just to see how you're doing," I lie. If I come out with my intentions now, she won't give me what I want. I've learnt that the hard way. She has to be the one to suggest it, I've gotta leave her a trail of breadcrumbs to pick up and lead her to my wolves den.

"For real?" She asks, this is where it gets tricky. If she smells bullshit I can never go here again…

"Yeah, it's been a while you know…" If I haven't got her now, I'll be able to reel her in with this, "All this time… It's got me thinking about… you… and what happened and…" Throw in COVID-19, "You know with this fucked up Corona shit, I can't stop—"

"—Elmo, I don't think this is a conversation to be having over a phone call, come over. Let's talk."

Hook, line and sinker. Works every fucking time. Damn. I'm good.

"When's a good time?" I ask, securing the bag.

"In an hour? Maybe two?"

"Calm, see you later b," I say.

"Laters," she says with her signature kissy sound, ending the call.

I'm having a blem again. The sun went down a while ago, a deep dark blue is staring back at me from the glass. I bring my down my blem, and look back at the daggers in the back of head. Dojo was glaring. The moment Doja opened the door to their flat, he was behind her, screwing me.

More like he'd like to screw me.

Oh well, I'm here for Doja, and a fuck. She was in the kitchen making dinner. Can't lie, I've missed her cooking but food isn't a priority. Never is.

I didn't expect to be served food before getting down and dirty, thought she'd wanna chat as soon as I got here but she greeted me and ushered me in, told me dinner was in fifteen.

It's already my third blem, should've figured she was lying. She's always lying but that's just her isn't it. She doesn't know what she wants, and as long as she stays like this I'll always have a way in.

Yeah, tonight won't be the last. It's been the same so far, like old times. Not like the last time, but it feels like how we used to chill— well minus Dojo… he'd normally just fuck off.

Dunno why he's still here but we move init.

Doja comes back and sets the table, steamy pasta in little white bowls. She always does pasta, this girl never changes. Dojo's already moved to the table, I finish off my blem before sitting down. She's particular about not smoking at the table but I leave my rolling shit on it nonetheless.

"Hmm… so good sis, you always make the best pasta," Dojo says after digging in. Doja's sat across from me and smiles at him warmly. She's such a woman. I don't know, but she's the type that's not like Oxi and the devil in the sandpit. You can tell she's kinda all there. You know. Probably why I was in the mood to fuck her tonight. I kinda miss it, need a refresher for my palette.

I scoff down some pasta.

"Elmo, how you liking it?" She asks me.

"It's alright."

"Just alright?"

"What, you fishing for compliments are we?"

"Maybe I am."

"Say it with your chest," I say.

She turns her head away from me to look at the table, "I am." She's blushing.

If Dojo wasn't screwing me before we started speaking, he probably is now. I glance at him and oh would you look at that he is. I laugh. Turning back to Doja, she looks like she's still waiting for me to say something.

"Pasta's pasta," I say. She looks pissed.

"For fuck's sake, Elmo," she says. She looks like she's about to cry. All pink with anger.

"What?"

"Are you serious?"

"What?"

"I thought— "

"You thought what?"

"I dunno, that Corona had made you change."

"Made me change?" I laugh.

"Oh you think it's funny do you?"

"That you're so gullible and stupid, yeah."

"That's what I get, right? For actually—"

"Oh not this again," I say putting down my spoon. If she starts yapping on about feelings and shit Imma need a fucking blem— nope strike that. Imma need to head the fuck out.

"Then what the fuck did you come here for then? I thought you wanted to talk?"

"Well, isn't the cat outta the bag? Why'd you think I came here?" I asked, she glared at me. I smirked. She knows why I came. Damn though if I'd just played along, said something about her *fucking* pasta then it wouldn't be happening like this. Who knows what she's gonna do now. Probably kick me the fuck out and Imma need to go back on Tinder or something… I dunno. Urgh, it's gonna be so long.

Shit. I've just fucked myself, haven't I?

Doja starts smiling. Her eyes start twinkling. She gets up and walks up behind Dojo, wrapping her arms around her brother. She brings her head down to sit on his shoulder, slowly. Her eyes drag themselves up from his collarbone.

They stop at me, and she licks her lips.

My stare intensifies. Is she doing what I think she's doing? Naaa.... *This can't be*. I never pegged her for a Lannister type bitch.

She's not about to become Cersei in this room, *right here, right now*...

She licks her brother's neck all the while looking at me.

Spoke too soon... *didn't I?* Guess you never really know anyone. Everyone's capable of moving mad no matter who they are.

This whole time I thought she was some sappy, I'm love in with you type girl, the I'm in touch with my feelings girl who only wears Y2K garms... Oh boy was I wrong.

She turns her head completely towards Dojo. He looks down at her, his eyes are pleading. He looks... confused... yet excited... Man these siblings are something else.

Some Game of Thrones type shit right here. Dojo's hand goes to the back of Doja's head, and pulls her face to his.

They're lipsing like it's no one's business. Well, their parents might have something to say but that ain't my issue now is it?

Doja pulls her head out of her brother's hands. She pulls out a chair from the dining table, and steps on it. "Alexa play Kitchen Kings by D Block Europe," she calls out. Moments later the music starts filtering into the room.

She looks down at her brother, me and then does something unexpected. She steps up onto the table and kicks *everything* to the floor.

Glasses of water smashing.

Pasta smacks the floor like a wet kiss.

Plates looking like pieces of a puzzle.

My rolling shit— gone.

She looks at me smiling, "Pasta's pasta, *right Elmo?*" She asks me, stretching her hand out to invite me.

This girl's crazy... but that means I can enjoy her more... *and* her brother. I'll make them my bitches.

I take her hand and step up onto the table. She looks at me up and down, before sliding out of her skirt. She raises her arms up straight, another invite. Can't this girl do anything? For fucks sake, whatever. It's a beat. My paws pull up her t-shirt over her head, her boobs hanging down in full view.

She smirks up at me before descending on her knees. Her hands wrap around the base of my furry red dick and she pulls me into her mouth cunt.

Slurp.

Moan— that's Doja by the way not me.

Bop.

"Dojo you just gonna sit there?" His mouth is open at the dining table, eyes transfixed on his sister. What an annoying little fucker, this is like any young boy's porno-filled dream yet here I am about to go limp.

Maybe it's because I know Doja's in love with me, tried to play hard to get and isn't really a spice.

SLURP, SLURP.

I mean come on, this blowjob is just fucking sloppy. Her teeth are everywhere. If I'd known she was this bad, I really wouldn't have gotten involved with her in the first place, *naaaa* seriously. It's long to teach someone how to be a better fuck.

Took me so long to clock just how shite she is because she was the girl with the feelings, the missionary with pussy. Not your average nun, naaaa she wears 2000's corsets as tops... *still*, but like you get me the fake missing spice girl. At the end of the day it's just pussy.

She lies back like a dead fish outta water. I go in and out, in and out. Couple moans here and there and it's like I just gave a bloody tuna CPR.

Cum, Cum, Resurrection.

CUUUUM.

Bish-bash-bosh, end of story.

Not gonna lie, she's been the only person I've been fucking nowadays that simps me like that, licking me all up in that flattery. It's kinda cute she sees the world like Walker's prawn cocktail crips. I eat, crack and snap her and she's still inside a pink-romance hued packet. Convenient, huh?

Sluuuurp.

But it got short lived real quick cause she realised I'm just there for the pussy, and honestly I couldn't give a shit.

SUCCCCTION.

Oh, and Dojo he's just sitting there— watching when he should be touching, if not me then at least do more than bloody watch— because it's fucking obvious he loves her in a Lannister type way, you get me.

And this blowjob is shit.

But these twins can't even do incestuous dinning table spice right, for fuck's sake.

I was having more fun in a fucking Weatherspoons toilet— hell— even at the police station. At least Dyer had balls bigger than a bloody fucking cashew.

Naaaa, fuck this I'm actually going limp.

Slurp.

"Dojo, mate roll me a blem—" I look down at my disappearing dick, she can feel it losing its steel, "—it looks like your sister is gonna kill my stiffy without one." He gets up and looks for the rolling stuff that dropped on the floor earlier.

Swirl.

I'm never gonna cum with this *shite*.

Doja bops her head to my tip and sucks hard. I wince, this isn't working. "Naaaa Doja get off I'm not feeling this."

PLOP.

Doja releases my dick, "Just gimme a couple minutes more I promise you—"

"—Naaa fuck off," I say, cutting her off. Her eyes are pleading up to me. Tearing up, like a sinner making her last confession to God.

A truly holy sight for Dojo, the nun spice on her knees praying to her red God to let her continue using what God gave her.

What I gave her, *inside*—in all our masses before— when I bestowed to her the blessing of my furry red fire. An addiction, a desire, with her wanton slobber hanging from the corners of her cunt. Sloppily drizzling, drowning her neck and breasts.

Glisteningly wet like the holy nun she is.

A hand comes to gently hold her prayer.

I smile down at her, and she kisses her God softly, with dignity and grace. I grab her halo and her eyes embrace me warmly, the hot tears washing away her sins.

A gentle stream flowing, from her eyes and lips to her furry red prayer. He soaks it all up kiss by kiss, washing away the sin, revealing his raw limp innocence.

Stroke.

Her hair is so soft, the strands slipping through mine. She leans into my red furry paw before bringing her other hand to my wrist.

Her eyes are begging me to follow her, to let her have what she wants. What God doesn't listen to his disciples asks?

She pulls my arm and her prayer, and I let her.

She gently tugs me from my perch on heaven, to her mortal coil. My knees slide onto the table on either side of her. She lets go of me completely.

Her hands slide to my hairy chest and she pushes me down fast and hard. In one split second…

BANG.

My back hits the dinning table.

My mouth opens a bit, lowkey feel a bit winded not gonna lie.

Blem.

I clamp my lips around it, and shift my head to see Dojo sparking it.

Inhale.

Dojo walks around to the opposite end of the table. He grabs Doja's hips and slides his hands down the sides. Before sliding up and hooking his fingers around her panties and dragging them down to the depths of hell.

I take the blem out of my mouth.

Doja rises up, above me, in-between me. A birds-eye view of her last supper. She smirks.

Bang.

Her body bends in the middle, hands at either side of my face. Downward dog, her boobs hanging like light bulbs from the roof in a house.

Exhale.

The smoke rising up through the triangle chimney of her planted hands and head. She whips her head back to look her brother, smiling at him.

Coaxing him with the full view of her pussy, she then steps out of the V of my legs and places her feet on ether side of my waist before sitting down on my stomach. Her hands slithering up me like a snake, a holy puppet-master pulls her strings straightening her back up into a straddle.

Preparing herself for a horse ride into the garden of Eden, she smirks.

Inhale.

She fists my red apples, her red prayer still limp.

Hands grab each of my feet roughly, and drag me and my holy passenger down the end of the table.

I can't see him, but I know it's Dojo.

My legs are spread further apart.

Exhale.

Fingers stroke around the rim of my arsehole. Doja circles her hips around the saddle of my stomach, wetting the fur.

Dojo licks up and down my entrance, before slipping his tongue in. Feeling himself around, wetting me and adds a finger.

I take another toke from my blem.

He adds another finger. Pumping in and out.

Another and then another.

Exhale.

He removes himself completely. I look up at Doja; she's looking down at me, her hair partly falling down from the sides of her head, partly stuck to her face, neck and breasts.

She's grinding.

Getting wetter.

Waiting.

I can feel Dojo softly pressing his head at my door. I bring my blem to my mouth.

He plunges in.

I gasp the smoke out, dropping the blem on the fur of my neck.

He starts thrusting.

I start screaming.

I've lost my blem. It's burning, I can see it turning me slowly from red to black. I'm burning—

I'm smoking.

Dojo hooks his hands under my butt, at the seams of my thighs and penetrates me harder.

"Ahhhh...."

Faster.

"Oh, *OuuH*," I become harder.

He thrusts deeper, and I'm HARD.

"*OooH, OuuuuH,*" I squirm.

In.

Moan.

Out.

Doja sinks down on me. "Shit, fuck… *meeeee,*" she gasps.

The blem bounces off my burnt fur.

"You… *bitch,*" Dojo grunts.

She laughs her head back, arching down to her spine, all the while grinding up and down on me.

Dojo penetrates me with more vigour, and RIPS fill the room.

Fuck this feels *waaaaaaay* too good.

Fuck, fuck, *"FUcccccCK."*

Liquid biology trickles down my butt crack.

"Doja… *AHHHH,*" Dojo grunts.

The slaps of sex are everywhere, filling the room like an injection of gas. Engulfing all of us through the rawness of our meat, drowning out whatever fucking song Alexa is playing right now.

In.

"Elmo…" Doja moans.

Out.

Another fucking moan from her.

IN.

I scream.

"Fuck… *YOU*," Dojo spits as his anger spills.

Overflowing—

OUT.

From it's familial constraints.

I rip. I bleed. I scream. I breathe.

I smile up at Doja, tears wetting the fur on my face. There's nothing left.

I'm finished, but the twins are still fucking me.

It hurts.

I feel like I'm ripping apart, like there'll be nothing left to fuck anymore. He thrusts harder, faster and calls out his sister's name.

IN.

I scream.

"Doja…. AHHH." He cums.

Breathless, Dojo PLOPS himself out and uncorks the bloody cum inside me.

Doja is riding my limp dick, sorrowfully and pitifully. Dojo looks like he's about to cry. His dick starts to rise up again at the naked sight of her. "*Sis…*" He whispers.

She ignores him and keeps looking at me.

He whimpers, and whines like a bitch.

Peak.

She can see I'm dead. My dick is so limp it just slips out of her.

He loves his sister and she couldn't give a shit. Love is so cruel it makes me laugh. He fucked her through me, but it's almost like she's erased him from her sight.

All she could see was *me*.

She was worshipping *me*.

But he was watching her back the whole time, coveting my faithful disciple.

I start laughing.

She's my bitch.

And I'm cackling like a witch.

Cause I don't give a shit about anything. It's not my issue, init.

Thank *fuck* for that.

EIGHT

I'm dead.

     The ceiling's living more than me right now. The light's flicking on and off. I don't have any spare bulbs but even if I did, I know I wouldn't be bothered anyways.

     I couldn't give two flying fucks.

     It took me so fucking long to get back to my shit-hole of a flat. Like those twins really killed me, took it out of me.

     My arsehole hurts like a bitch. I died, I actually died. It feels like I'm betraying myself when I replay the scenes of last night in my mind. I didn't cum. I wasn't feeling the best exactly… but I was feeling nothing and pain… *but I liked it?*

     Is this what my bitches feel like? Is this what Apollo felt like when I rammed into him? Life is full of surprises. We always be walking a tight fucking rope across a sea but what's life without a little spice? A little danger? A little pain?

     Would I be asking myself this if I didn't get fucked into oblivion last night, cum-free? Naaa, I don't think I would be. This is just how it is, how life goes. It goes round and round, in and out of holes. Swims through desire and pleasure. Fucks with you, fucks for you, fucks in you.

     Ding. DA. Ding. DA. Ding.

I need a blem and a drink.

Ding. DA. Ding. DA. Ding.

Fuck's sake, the fuck is that? I look in the direction of the sound. The kitchen. Damn, it's Mazzy's trap phone. He's my mate, and I like that he's my mate — but he always chooses the wrong fucking times to bell me. Cause I can't be bothered to go get it.

The phone just carries on ringing till it dies. I'm still lying here, on the dirty floor of my living room, dying too.

I kinda don't get it though.

As I'm laying here on my manky floor, I hear more. It sounds like there's shit building, maybe footsteps maybe something else.

BANG.

The fuck was that?

BANG, BANG.

Bodies pile in. Sounds like a clattering of limbs, TRASH. Something?— More like someone has fallen down on my living room floor, at my feet.

I raise my head to see a short mane of blue hair. Oxi. What was she doing here? My eyes follow down her body to the doorway she burst in through, and oh *what a surprise...* Jezza.

"What the fuck are you two doing here?" I ask. Oxi looks like she's about to open her mouth to respond, "Get out— right now— both of you!"

"Elmo— " Jezza starts.

"GET OUT!" I shout.

"We came to say we're sorry," Oxi says.

I turn my head to her, she recoils her head slightly back when my eyes land on her completely. Like a vampire shying away from the sun, "And you think saying 'sorry' is gonna cut it, yeah?"

Silence.

"Give me a fucking break, you two are unbelievable. I should've never swiped on you— all this shit would've never happened." I say and Oxi gives me a hard look sitting up and adjusts her glasses.

Look at her just chilling there. Damn, I really need to get my door fixed.

"Of course just saying sorry isn't gonna cut it— words are worthless, meaningless. We came to show you we're sorry."

Like I give a shit about the fact they left me in shit with the feds. Like I don't really care. They care— obviously or they wouldn't be here. Nor would Jezza have tried to talk to me on the phone yesterday either.

"And what if I don't wanna hear or see it?" I ask, my tone leaving her dumbfounded there for a second.

"You— Elmo— one of the most skits people I know… *You're gonna say no* to free blems, zoots, alcohol *and* a good time? *Really?*"

I just look at her, then turn to look at Jezza in the doorway, he's holding two Sainsbury's bags and I can see the shapes of bottles piercing through.

Damn. They got me. How'd they know me so damn well though? That's kinda fucking creepy because I don't know jack-shit about them. Well, maybe just how much Oxi likes to cum and have a zoot. Oh, and how Jezza's got some sorta soft spot for her.

"Elmo…?" Jezza asks, he's like a little puppy by the doorway. He's too hesitant to even come inside unless he's been invited in. He invited himself to my number and my call log, but can't come inside? I swear that fucked up morning when I lost the bomb and we got arrested I had cum coming outta my butt— and it's not like I can bend my own dick into my arsehole and fuck myself. It was *probably* him. He even dropped me in it with the cops, and made me a *snitch* and he's acting like a little yute *here*?

Makes me fucking laugh and laugh some more. My head hits the floor again.

THUD.

Ah it's the ceiling again. Manky shit, not gonna lie.

"Elmo…" Jezza starts.

Oh yeah forgot about them for a second, "Yeah sure come in, init. You're already here."

"You sure— you probably hate us."

"I don't care enough to hate— probably should, but let's face it, I really can't be bothered. Just come in before I change my fucking mind." I say. I hear him step inside and close the door behind him.

Doesn't matter anyways, it's not like the lock works. At this rate, that shit's just for show init.

"You gonna get up Elmo?" Oxi asks.

"Can't be asked."

"Ahhh come on, you can't lay there forever, you're lying between the sofa and the coffee table. Like where we gonna put shit apart from the table? Cause I wanna sit on the sofa and put my feet where your belly is," she whines.

I turn to her. "Fuck off Oxi, I can lay where I want. This is *my* flat. If I wanna lay here I will. You wanna sit there— go ahead— *I don't care*." I say.

She raises her eyebrows and shrugs her shoulders before pushing herself off the floor. She throws herself onto the sofa and then one by one puts the soles of her Chelsea boots on my red furry carpet of a stomach.

Fuck. Maybe I should've tried harder to move. This hurts a little. Oh well, c'est la vie. I dunno where Jezza's chilling but from wherever he is, he passes the Sainsbury's bags to Oxi and she plops them on the table.

"Blem?" She asks, looking down at me. She took the word right outta my mouth.

"Yes."

"Yes?" She asks. What is she deaf?

"YES, YES." I shout. She smiles and starts rolling.

"Elmo… " Jezza starts, but I'm still watching the ceiling. Wish there was some music or something… wish I could have an Alexa right about now because I can't be bothered for anything but I'm too broke for that. "ELMO!"

"What?" I hiss.

"Here," Oxi says handing me a blem and lighter. I light it and take a drag. It feels so good to smoke right now, it even cancels out her boots using my belly as a footstool.

It doesn't take long for me to smell weed in the room. One of them's sparked a zoot no doubt. They're also talking about something but I'm not gonna lie, I'm zoning out because I'm not listening to a bloody word.

Did I even sleep since the twins place?

Sleep…

I don't even remember the last time I *actually* slept.

Shit… Is that bad… that's gotta be bad right? But then again people don't assume I'm a crackhead for nothing— although I ain't a fan of crack, to be honest that shit's wack. As wack as people who like doing G, now that's a certified way to accidentally overdose.

"Elmo?" I look over at Jezza, and he's looking at me like he's waiting, buzzing like a follow request.

"I zoned out there, not gonna lie— what you asking me?"

"Are you blind?" He asks. "Do you want a drink?" I look down at his out stretched hand with a bottle of open red wine in it.

O, I feel kinda dumb right now. Guess this happens when you get spacey. Damn, I must be fucking tired to not realise wagwan— can you imagine?

I'm not even the high one right now.

Well, technically all the windows in this grimy living room are closed and I think they're on like zoot number 3 or 4. Can you even get high off the weed in a hot-boxed room? Even if you could it doesn't really work unless you've been smoking too. Well, *speaking from experience*.

I sit up, Oxi's legs falling down from me as I get up. No more red fluffy footstool for her, yeah fuck that shit. I walk around to the opposite side of the sofa where she's sat, the coffee table between us. I stick out my paw to the right of me, where Jezza's sat cross legged.

He hands me the bottle and I take a much needed swig. "Whose got the zoot?" I ask.

"I do," Oxi says.

"Pass it here," she takes one last toke before giving it to me.

Inhale.

Silence.

Exhale.

I look at both of them. They're just watching me smoke like a bunch of CCTV cameras. "What were you guys talking about?"

Inhale.

"Well you missed quite a lot actually—"

Exhale.

"—No, he didn't Oxi," Jezza turns to me, red-faced. "You didn't, honestly."

"Oh yeah? Then why so pink, Jezza?" I ask with a smirk, Oxi bursts out laughing.

Inhale.

"I'm what?" He asks panicked, touching his cheeks with his hands.

Exhale.

"You're blushing!" Oxi says while she's motioning for me to pass her the bottle. I take a quick swig before I put it on the coffee table between us.

"What were you lot talking about then, come on," I coax, and Oxi takes a long swig.

"Jezza was telling me about how he tried to fuck some girl, he brought her home the other day and she must've told him it wasn't happening when she saw his dick size—" She starts laughing, "—Then to top it all off— he—" She starts laughing some more, so much more that there's tears coming out of her eyes, "—He couldn't even get it up."

I look at Jezza and offer him the zoot, "That's deep man, not gonna lie."

He takes the zoot from me, and looks up at the ceiling taking a long drag.

"Damn, though mate that's gotta be rough… has that happened to you before?"

"Nah of course it hasn't, that was the first time," Jezza answers.

"*Oh yeah?*" I ask, struggling to hold in my laugh. I take another swig from the bottle Oxi just gave me again, this is starting to get good.

"*You lying piece of shit!*— You told me the other month that you couldn't get it up with some girl you met at work," Oxi interrupts.

"Did you just say work—" I say, turning towards Jezza, "You have a job? Doing what? I can imagine you being a pencil-pusher, explains why you're so wound up with your shit. You can't even tell the love of your life— that she's the love of your life. That's just sad and pathetic, but the pencil-pusher part would totally make *all that* make hella sense."

"*The love of my life?*" Jezza whispers. He looks like he's in shock. It's almost like his whole world of delusions just came crashing down. Yikes, doesn't he realise it's fucking obvious that he's in love with Oxi?

"The love of Jezza's life? Since when was there someone like that around?" Oxi asks, she turns and faces Jezza, looking him square in the eyes. "It better not be me."

Oh boy, man just got rejected before he could even pull the bloody net out from the sea of fish. Don't worry mate, there's plenty more fish in the sea— isn't that what they say? I may be now starting to understand why he kept it to himself… but oh well. What's done is done, can't really be undone now, aye.

And… now that it's done, I might as well follow through with it, and see how far I can push his dreams out there…

"*Ooooh, Oxiiii*—" I sing, " —it was you I was referring to the whole time and you know it. Playing

73

dumb isn't hot you know," I finish and she sniggers at me.

"Well, then you know I'm playing dumb because I—" She starts.

"—What?"

"— I— I don't fucking know, okay?" She exclaims, frustrated. I give her the bottle.

"GUYS," Jezza shouts, grabbing all of our attention, "You know I'm still here right? I can hear everything you's are saying—"

"—Jezza I'm well aware of that. It wasn't like you were ever gonna come clean now, is it?" I cut in.

"You don't know that."

"Well, then. When were you gonna do it? Tell Oxi you liked her or loved her or whatever?" I ask and from the corner of my eye I can see Oxi taking a right long swig from the bottle.

"I don't wanna say this right now, Elmo. *Come on man*," he pleads. He looks like he wants to bury his head in the sand and wiggle his butt in the air, almost like some dramatic traffic light signal flashing to get the hell away from him. A coward, huh? Well... that's only human.

"Jezza we wouldn't have worked anyway." Oxi chimes in.

"What do you mean?" Jezza asks.

"Like, I dunno exactly but I just know it wouldn't have. You get me?" Oxi responds.

"No, I don't get you."

"Aw come on, be real. Wake up. You don't really like me *like that*... you're just confused because I'm *here* and *I've always been here*."

"No, I— I do *like like* you, Oxi."

"Jezza, this is what guys do. I don't know but like…"

"See, you just said so yourself. *You don't know.*"

"Aren't you both just a bunch of idiots," I say shaking my head. I need a fucking blem the way this conversation is going, really seems like it's on the verge of awkward but also lowkey kinda getting somewhere but simultaneously not.

"Oi, I'm not an idiot! Can't speak for Jezza though," Oxi replies.

"I'm an idiot," Jezza confirms.

"Wow, something we agree on there, Jezza," I say.

"Bruv, is it everyday come for me yeah?"

"Well… If I didn't you wouldn't be here finally having some sort of conversation with Oxi about how you feel, now would ya?"

"Errrrrr Elmo, you're soooo jarring man. You've humiliated me you know," he says.

I sit down, legs crossed by the coffee table and grab the rolling stuff. "I know mate, but life is life. What can I say?"

"Err what about being less of a dick, Elmo?"

"Isn't honesty the best policy?" I say, halfway done with rolling the blem.

"He's right Jezza," Oxi begins, "If Elmo hadn't exposed you, who knows when you would've done it yourself." She leans over the coffee table, her hand stroking Jezza's cheek, "Because now I can prove to you why we wouldn't work".

Jezza gulps.

I take a drag of my blem and Oxi places a slow soft kiss on his other cheek.

Oooooh boy.

Oooooh boy.

If Jezza was nervous before— now his head's probably running into overdrive on loan from overtime. I can't tell if she's just gonna play with him or actually try to fuck him but we'll see, init. I'm bringing my blem back up to face to stop myself from laughing right now. That would completely kill whatever this is— and I wanna see this play out. Jezza looks like he's either about to piss himself or experience curry-stinging diarrhoea.

Inhale.

Oxi moves her mouth to Jezza's, running her tongue around his lips.

Exhale.

She pushes his mouth open, and starts full on lipsing him.

Inhale.

Jezza's started running his hands up and down her, like a hungry animal starving for more. Pressing at her sides, hard. I can see the dip of his fingers on her skin through her top. She lets herself be taken by his need, his wanton desire for her, that she's crawling completely like some demon from the sofa, to the coffee table. Her body pressing on the coffee table, her feet hanging off.

My blem's finished.

THUD.

The rolling stuff, Sainsbury's bag of bottles and the open bottle has fallen to the floor. Instantly I'm reaching out for the rolling stuff, luckily it's all inside the pouch but I wipe it on myself for good measure. That can't get wet.

Drip.

Too bad for the rest of the table and floor though, the alcohol is dripping off the edge.

Oxi keeps writhing on the table. Jezza's lips still connected to hers. Her hands on his shoulders and presses on them.

I start rolling a zoot.

Oxi slides completely off the table and onto Jezza. He's so fucking flimsy, his back gives out onto the floor like metro newspapers on the tube. She drags her torso up and pulls her top up and over her head. Then she flings it to the door in front of them. I can see Jezza's face inside the triangles of her limbs with his.

A deer in headlights that's what he is. Like the one that gets killed at the beginning of Jordan Peele's Get Out. Damn… I loved that film.

I just finished billing the zoot.

But onto the point, he's gonna get killed like that deer. I can feel it— the moment of truth is coming soon… it looks Oxi's gonna actually try to fuck him.

She's grinding herself up his legs.

Inhale.

Oxi's hands grab the waistband of his jeans. She unzips them and she grabs his dick. Jezza starts moaning.

Exhale.

"I'm gonna fuck you now," Oxi says.

Inhale.

Jezza's head slowly raises from the floor, "Uh huh………*yeaaaaaah….*" Jezza sounds like a crackhead walking around in some random cloud level in a Mario game. Oxi completely brings down his briefs and jeans, his hard dick standing and waiting.

Exhale.

Oxi positions herself above his dick, and slides down.

Huh?

I'm blinking harder right now.

Did—did I just see that right? Fuck, how high am I right now? I shoo away the smoke clouds from my zoot covering my vision. Oxi's still straddling him, there's no space between her cunt and his dick. I must've been seeing things… *right?* Damn, what strain is this weed? Must be a Cali one.

Oxi lifts herself up.

Jezza's dick is lying limp like a dead fish.

I'm dead, but not as dead as him though.

I'm laughing. The dick didn't even go in…

So I *did* just see that right…

Well, damn… that's a first because I've never seen something like *that* before. When Oxi was going down, it looked like Jezza's dick was bending down at the same time too. How can his dick just instantly go and start limping down when she was sinking down… imagine, his dick could've been *drinking*.

What.

A.

Shame.

78

"See, Jezza this is why we'd never work," Oxi says.

Silence.

Jezza's just looking up at the ceiling not saying a word. Just the slowest tears I've ever seen coming down his face. If he didn't wanna fail her little test all he had to do was cum. I mean— *seriously?*

Pathetic.

I hold out the zoot in their un-sexual general direction, "Anyone want the zoot?"

NINE

Not gonna lie though, what an interesting confession. Normally someone just gets rejected like you know, that's cool that you like me but it ain't got nothing to do with me mate.

Oxi though... now she may have gone *aaaaa bit* too far, but it was well worth it in the end. If Jezza hasn't got the message now— he never will.

They're both gone now and I'm still in the living room, chilling, smoking. The usual.

Ding. DA. Ding. DA. Ding.

Ah, it's the trap phone. Might as well get up now and see what Mazzy wants. I walk to the kitchen. I see the tin bread box vibrating on the counter.

Ding. DA. Ding. DA. Ding.

Jesus. These brick Nokia phones are just made of power, aren't they? I open the box and pick up the brick.

"Yo, wagwan Mazzy?"

"*Yo, wagwan?* Seriously Elmo? I've been tryna fucking call you for the longest time. *Longer than the drag it took Eastenders to reveal who murdered fucking Lucy Beale.*"

"You watch that?"

"Naaa I dropped it when the Mitchell's basically just weren't there."

"Phil's still there—"

"—Well don't YOU just have sooo much FUCKING time. Anyways—"

"—Anyways, Eastenders isn't—"

"—It's shit."

"Mazzy…"

"Elmo, would it kill you to pick up the fucking phone?" Silence. I don't really have anything to say. He knows that I know the answer. "Okay, so we're going to Paris."

"What? For what?"

"For the job."

"What job?"

"The BoJo one."

"Why do we need to trek to France though? He's in London, mate."

"I'm not getting into details over the phone. Just know one thing. We're getting a new one— that's all you need to know for now."

"A new what?"

"Bomb, you shitty red fucker."

"You know I've still got the other one from before— from the airport," I say. Mazzy kisses his teeth thru the phone.

"Elmo, mate… You and I know both know that's a lie." Fuck, fuck, fuck.

"Naaaa it's not," I try.

"Bruv, cut the shit. You lost it. You think I don't know you by now. When you were taken by the feds they would've found it and charged you *blah, blah, blah...* if you'd had it. Doesn't take a genius to figure out why you're not in prison right now, Elmo. You didn't have it then, meaning you don't have it now."

"I have it, I hid it."

"Elmo, mate. The plan was never for you to even have to hide it you know or even have it for that long. You were meant to use it then. Can't help it that Corona just came and fucked everything up you know. Like, come on mate, you can't even hide a fucking hard on, you want me to believe you can hide a bomb from the fucking feds? Who do you think I am—"

"—You're Mazzy, my maaaaate. Who knows that I'm—"

"—I wasn't born yesterday, Elmo. You don't have it, let's not long this out— I've got shit to do before we head to France," he says.

Silence.

"Okay, okay you got me. But like… *do they know…?*"

"That you lost it? No, if they found that out on top of you being caught by the feds and snitching—- we'd *both* be dead."

"Okay so, this you, yeah? Your people— Paris."

"Yeah," he says.

"Okay, so when we heading?"

"Tonight, be ready. I'll come for you."

"Tonight, ditto." Looks I'm going to Paris. Would you look at that. I wanna make Paris a little bit of fun though. Can't be all work and no play. I'm gonna go and charge my actual phone so I can use Tinder in the so-called *city of love*.

It's not long before the buzzer at the door is ringing and I walk out the front door to him. I hop into his car and he speeds the fuck out of my street. He turns his head to me, "You got anything with you?" He asks.

"Well apart from my passport, nope. I don't really need anything."

"You sure? Might be a couple of nights— we could stop at a Primark or something and get you some clothes," he says.

"What am I? Your bitch? I don't think so."

"Aw come on man, I'm just tryna help you out," he says with a strange smile. Why he's smiling in this situation— I don't bloody know.

"That's what you always do— help me out— even when I don't ask."

"Come on, Elmo don't be ungrateful. I've done a lot for you. Don't throw it in my face."

"You don't own me," I say looking at the road, we're leaving Greater London.

"That's true for sure, but *they* own us."

"Well, it is what it is, can't be helped now, can it?"

"We gotta make it out of this alive. After all this shit I've been through," he says turning to look at the road ahead of him. When I first met Mazzy he was just a local dealer having motives at his place. I'm not even sure when he got involved with them, could've even been before we met— but that was years ago. Mazzy used to be a God on the decks back in those days. His motives were the shit; all the gear you could want, blasting music and people looking for a good fuck every three steps, in every room. I guess life just got in the way of the motive life for him. I certainly wouldn't want what's on his shoulders, that's for sure.

"What's this shit you speak of?"

He turns to look at me, one hand on the wheel. "Seriously, Elmo?" I smile. His nostrils flare up, "You shitty prick."

"But you love me," I say.

SCREEEEECH.

The car comes to a halt.

THUD.

My head bangs forward, hard. Ouch, that fucking hurts. My paw comes to my forehead. Damp, it's fucking damp, my fur is damp. Did this fucker just make me bleed?

"Why THE FUCK did you do that?" I shout.

"Are you crazy, Elmo?"

"Me? You're asking *me* if I'm crazy? I should be asking you that— bloody stopping the car in the middle of a fucking motorway— if you don't start moving people are—"

"—You stupid, deluded motherfucker—"

"—if you don't start moving, the fucking cars are gonna start bleeping, mate— have you seen those crazy road rage memes like, mate— and in London, bruv— you're messing with some scary people—"

"—I DON'T GIVE A SHIT, ELMO." He screams, and I shut the fuck up. I don't remember the last time he was *this* angry. Fuck, this is bad. "What am I to you, Elmo?" He stares at me, deadpan. "Seriously. In that messed up head of yours, what am I?"

I laugh. He starts screwing me with his eyes and I can't help it. I know Mazzy... I just know it'll just piss

84

him off but I can't help it. I laugh harder. I start cackling like a whale on crack. My eyes close from the tears forming in my laughter, that is, until I hear some witch-like chanting. Like someone trying cast some witchy, juju spell— you can't help but open your eyes, can't ya?

To my surprise, there's no witch. It's Mazzy,

"GET. OUT. GET. OUT. GET. OUT. GET. OUT. GET. OUT. GET. OUT. GET. OUT. GET. OUT. GET. OUT. *GET THE FUCK OUT, ELMO!*"

Woah, he needs to chill.

I spot a box of straights in his glove compartment, and spark one.

CLICK.

As the smoke clears from my exhale, I see the opened door. When the fuck did his hand reach over to open the door and unbuckle my seatbelt? O shit, that's right— I never put on my seatbelt in the first place. Fuck, fuck, fuck? Am I losing it? How did I not notice him opening the door though? I'm not blind and he's not made of magic.

"Get THE FUCK out, Elmo." I'm looking between the open door and him, rounding back again and again with the same routine. Is he serious? Is he actually— does he actually want me to go?

A dry laugh escapes my mouth the second it opens to speak, I cough covering my mouth and throw the half smoked straight out the window. I look at Mazzy, "Mate—"

"—*Mate?*" He interrupts, with the dirtiest look I've ever seen on his face.

"Y-You know… it was a joke. Right? Come on, man. It just went too far, *you know me.*"

"*I, know you?*" Now he's the one laughing. "Don't you realise, Elmo? That I haven't known you for a long time now. I don't know who you are anymore.

You changed, and that's cool. We just work together, you're a colleague."

Ha, colleague my ass. Mazzy really thinks I was born yesterday. Like sure, I might've lost a few brain cells here and there— one too many lines, a few too many nights ago—no, forget that— years ago.

My eyebrow raises, "So... you're gonna risk your life for a colleague, yeah? If you're gonna lie, then make it fucking believe-able— you twat."

"So answer the question, you never answered. What am I to you?"

"Bruv, you really need to ask? Isn't it obvious?"

"Well, naaaa, clearly fucking not. Why don't you enlighten the bloody class, why don't you?"

"You're my mate, Mazzy. *My friend.*"

"*Friend*," he repeats.

"*Bruv,* come on— *of course* you're my friend," I say with a smile. I'm about to put my arm over his shoulders but I don't think that'd be a good idea.

Silence.

"When's the last time we hung out? Huh, come now tell me— since you're soooo chatty and have all the fucking answers," he says.

Fuck. Fuck. Fuck.

I'm trying to think back, and *hard.* To be honest, I don't remember. I've got nothing. I—

"Exactly, Elmo."

Silence.

Clearly the discombobulated look on my face did the talking, "Exactly, Elmo."

I don't get it though, he's trying to say we're not friends anymore, but we are. I remember the good times, years ago. Although I just can't remember the last time we were actually chilling, you know— in the same room. Sure I admit, it's been a while… but I never— I never realised—

I don't get it.

"Then how comes you saved my fur? You saved my life." Mazzy just stares into my eyes. It's burning. His eyes, they're fucking burning through me. I don't know much longer I can do this… sit through this conversation.

I can feel the sweat in my butt-cheeks. My legs start twitching. I wasn't even this twitchy when I was being interrogated by the fucking feds, for fucks sake.

"If I'd known you'd be whatever *this* is— what you are now— I never would've got you into this world in the first place. You— the you from before that is— the you I was friends with, that's who I cared about, and it's for that guilt of mine, for *that* you, that I do what I do for you now. The thing is Elmo, I just don't know who you are anymore. You piss me off, but you always did… However, it's just not the same anymore. Maybe I've got some kinda fucked up duty towards you, or whatever, but to see what you've become— I… I don't know, man. These days all you do is disappoint me, in some sort of way… I'm kind of sorry, Elmo. But you broke the last straw, man. You really did. I put my neck on the line for you, time and time again and you just throw it back in my face. That's not a friend. You're a shitty person, Elmo. The shittest."

I don't know what to say. I push the door open wider and get out of the car. I fucked up. I fucked up real-time, and I don't even know when it all started to go wrong with Mazzy. Well, losing the bomb didn't help. Getting in it with the feds didn't either. Pissing him off in general didn't either— that much I know.

Fuck.

Did I just lose an *actual* friend? *Did I just lose Mazzy?*

Wait, do I actually…

Care?

For fucks sake, what am I? A sappy pussy? Why am I acting up like this? Why don't I just go back in and tell him to fuck off? Huh? That he's just chatting shit—

Maybe… *maybe*… it's because I know— I know this sinking feeling— he's—

NO! I slap myself. I need to wake the fuck up, and snap the fuck outta this.

WHAT THE FUCK IS WRONG WITH ME?

Clearly a lot, huh?

BEEP. HONK. BEEP. HONK.

I look around and realise, this whole time the cars behind us are moving mad like some damn orchestra— but there's obviously no movement, clearly because… *Mummy and Daddy are fighting again…*

Some bald guy sticks his head out of the driver's window, "Get out of the fucking road, you wanker!" He shouts. I give him the middle finger because boo-fucking-who, baldy.

He can fuck off.

BLEEEEEEEEEP.

The sea of cars go *off*. The cars have probably been going crazy this whole time— *see*, I told Mazzy. That idiot… but it's not like I even clocked this was happening either though. I was too wrapped up dealing with Mazzy and his fucking man-period.

They're mad— Mazzy's period's. The cars beeping and honking into oblivion… Aaaaah shit, I can't help but smile.

"ALRIGHT, THAT'S IT YOU FUCKER, I'M GONNA SHOW YOU WHERE THE SUN DON'T FUCKING SHINE," the bald guy shouts. He gets out of the car and punches me.

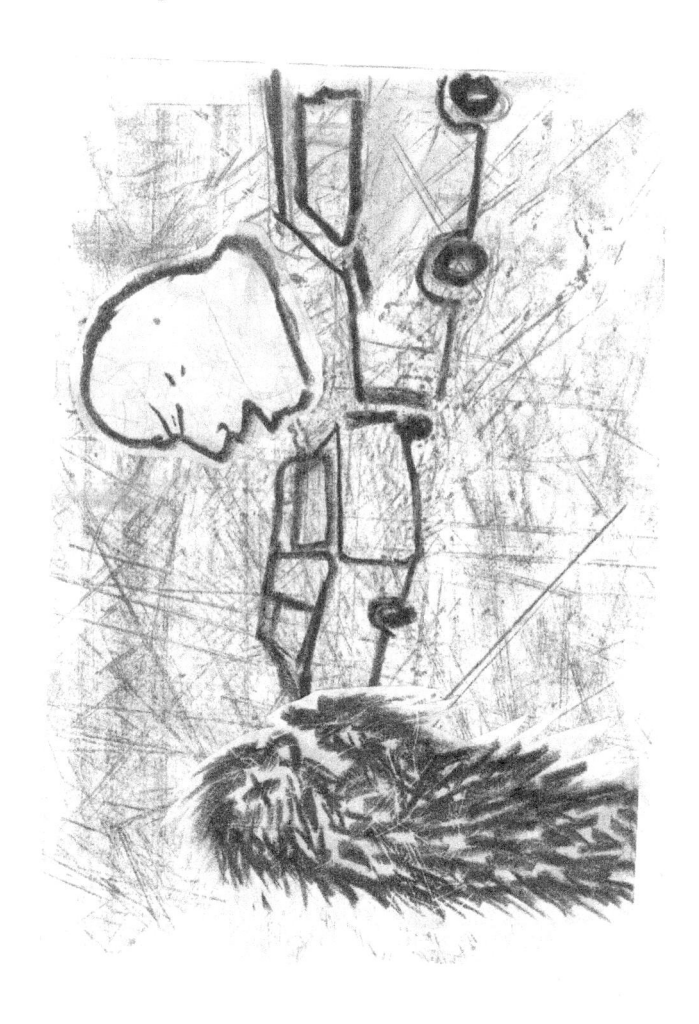

HOOOOOOOONK. HOOOOOOOONK. HOOOOOOOONK.

O, looks like it's *celeBRAtion time, come ON.* I start laughing, I just can't help it, I'm a fucking joker, man. Baldy thinks so too because looks like he's coming for another swing at me.

"Elmo!" Mazzy shouts, his head popping out from the car. "Get in the bloody car."

"Thought you told me to get out."

"Get in the fucking car, Elmo."

"Naaa, I'm not your bitch. You don't tell me what to do. You're not my fucking dad," I spit.

"Get in the car, bruv." Mazzy says.

"Listen to your mate, get in the car wanker," the baldy adds. I give a nice big middle finger.

"Naaa, what the fuck is this Mazzy? Huh, what type of games you playing here? You wilding out? Should you even be fucking driving right now?"

"Cut the shit, Elmo. Get in— you've got a job to do."

"It's always about the fucking job, huh? THE JOB's made you come to your bloody senses, huh? Well, that's just fucking great, init?"

"Get in," he says.

"For fucks sake," I mutter and get back in the car, baldy's second incoming punch just missing me as I duck into the tin box on wheels.

Once I close the door, Mazzy starts speeding off and we're back on track to go Dover and catch that ferry to France.

"So... *we cool?*" I ask.

Silence.

Fuck. I've really fucked things, huh.

Mazzy puts on the radio, usual bullshit pop playing. The most up-beat tweeney bop music on this sombre mood in the car just ain't it. All I wanna do is get out of here and onto the streets of Paris. One thing I am hoping is having time to have a little bit of fun here and there. All work and no play— that's Mazzy but all play and no work, now that's just a little bit of me.

I need to remind Mazzy how fun it is to be with me. *Mazzy, mate don't you worry*. Elmo's gonna remind you who the real Santa is, and here's a hint: he's red and furry.

It's been a couple hours, since we got to France. We've been driving through deserted French streets and Mazzy hasn't said a word since the motorway in the UK. The only thing that's been keeping me going through this shitty mood is smoking blems out the window of the car.

Never thought I'd be saying this, but Paris seems so dead at the moment. Everything looks shut. What happened to all the fun bars that used to make this city rival London's nightlife. Bruv, I should've stayed in London. At least I'd be hella fucked right now.

"Wagwan with Paris right now?" I ask, "Everything's shut and there's no one on the streets."

"Don't you read the news?"

"Naaa, tell me wagwan then," I say.

"France has some next up lockdown right now, and there's a 6pm curfew. Pretty sure the only businesses running at the moment are food stuff like supermarkets and that," he says looking at some street name above. Can't blame him squinting, it's fucking dark.

"You really should've said, man. Where we gonna have fun then?"

"Have fun? Elmo. We came here for a job— because of *your* fuck up."

"Jeeze man, chill. I get it. I'm the devil— *blah, blah, blah*. I'm tired."

"You're tired? What about me, *huh?* How'd you think I am?"

"Dandy."

"Sure, I'm dandy. *Just fucking dandy,*" Mazzy says, stopping the car. He gets out and I open the car door to get out from the passenger side. "Stay in the car."

"What?"

"I said, stay in the car."

"Bruv, if I'm staying in the car— what's the fucking point of me being here? How comes you fucking forced me to trek with you to France, then? *Bloody time-waster—*"

"—Just stay in the car. I'll come get you in a sec," he finishes. O, now that makes sense. He's checking on his people.

"Calm then. I'll stay in the car," I say and close the passenger door again. I watch Mazzy leave, close his door behind him, then cross the street. Looks like he's waiting at a door but I can't really see from here, then a couple minutes later he goes inside.

Great.

Now I'm really bored. I wonder how long mans is gonna take in there. It's not everyday, moving like he's some sorta fucking spy, for fucks sake.

I start snooping, like some nosy neighbour in all the compartments of the car. There's gotta be something here, it's Mazzy's car, for fucks sake.

Tissues, water bottle, baggy—

Hang on, *BAGGY!* Please, *please* tell me there's something in there. I'm holding it up, but I can't see anything. I open it up and dip my tongue inside the plastic like it's pussy— and *walaaah*.

Charlie.

Just as quickly as I swallowed the last crumbs, I'm already aching for more. Damn, I love me some good old shitty London coke. I need more, like now.

Unfortunately for me, what I get is Mazzy knocking on the window and some next up hand signals. He's telling me to get out and follow him init.

I get out. "Mazzy, do I look like special ops to you? You know I don't play C.O.D. It's not everyday solider talk, bruv."

"Common sense, though. You got out, nah? That's what I wanted." We get to a door, and he knocks three times. The door opens, slightly ajar, "It's me."

The door opens fully and we scuffle inside, I close the door behind me. Common sense, as Mazzy proved seconds ago— that I possess. The inside is dimly lit in the hallway, as we're walking past closed doors I can hear people speaking French, not that I understand a word of it though. I follow Mazzy into a room at the end, where he fist bumps some guy.

Mazzy steps aside, now I can see this guy better. He's looking at me and I'm looking at him. There's another guy fiddling with trap phones and calling cards on the table, bare duffle bags filled to the brim with cash wads. The guy steps toward me.

CLICK. CLACK.

I look to the sound, a guy on the table is messing with a gun. I gulp. Fuck, fuck, fuck. Mazzy knows some scary people. Although I always knew it wasn't fucking unicorns, I guess Mazzy was always my middle man— I'm starting to really to hate the fact it's come to *this*.

I'm as still as the sea after a storm. I don't wanna move, or make *one wrong* move. Anything really. I'm just starting to deep fucking mad this is.

"So, this is the guy?" He asks.

"Yeah, Elmo," Mazzy says.

The guy holds his hand out to me, "Richard." Hmm… British accent, of course Mazzy's connect is a Brit— although a Frenchie would've been more exciting, not gonna lie.

I shake his hand, "Elmo." God, I'm so fucking stiff. I go to bring my paw back, but he tightens his grip on me.

"So you're the crazy fucker that's gonna get the Prime Minister," he says. I can feel the blood rushing to my paw.

Is he tryna cut off my circulation? I didn't realise you could get amputated from a fucking handshake— because that's where this is heading if he doesn't let —the fuck—go.

"Yeah, that's the plan at least," I say, slowly. He just stares at me. I feel like he's sizing me up, ironic though since I'm taller than him. Although didn't they say El Chapo was a short man, 5'6 or something? I can't figure out where in the food chain this guy sits, but one thing's for sure— I get the feeling he's not someone you wanna mess with.

I've gotta keep myself in check.

Oh boy. At least the Charlie I had in the car will help straighten me out, and keep myself together… *hopefully.*

"Why?"

"Why?" I repeat. What's he on about?

"Why are you doing this?" He asks.

O, shit. This is a test, this is a *real* test. Failure could mean a coffin for me. Do I really wanna kill Boris?

Well…

"For the shit's and giggles," I laugh. O and the fact I have to or I'll be dead… Fuck, my laugh is starting to get louder.

I don't know why but this is kinda funny… How I even ended up mixed up in all this over some stupid minuscule thing but then me being me, gets roped into one fucked thing and to another.

Fuck. I really am stupid— and now I'm cackling, I feel the tears about to spill from my eyes.

"You're nuts," Richard smiles, "But I like you." He lets go of my hand. Well thank fuck for that, huh?

"Come by in 24 hours for pick up," he tells Mazzy.

"Ditto," he says and leaves. I follow him out of the room and out the fucking front door.

The second we're sat safely in the car, my body releases it's stiffness as I slouch into the seat. I let out the biggest breath I didn't know I was holding.

PISSSSSSSSSSS.

And another thing I didn't know I was holding… oops.

"For fuck's sake Elmo, don't pee in my car— there's a bloody street for that!"

TEN

Mazzy was rolling a zoot, and I was taking another swig at the red wine we brought. Mazzy booked an Airbnb last minute for tonight. We need to leave tomorrow night but we have no car at the moment.

What happened?

Mazzy left it at a garage nearby from the supermarket. Since it's closed and all, the job will be done tomorrow. The job— that is to extract evidence of my peeing escapade earlier.

What? Judgement ain't welcome here... Bruv.

Clearly those fuckers were some scary fucking people, for to be peeing myself like some wimp. I don't even blame myself like, for real. I feel like if I wasn't on Charlie when we were in there... I'm not sure I'd be alive right now...

Well now that we've got some downtime, I do wanna find something fun to do. If bloody COVID-19 wasn't a thing I'd just go to bar or something and drag Mazzy along. Like I wanna go see if the Moulin Rouge actually exists.

Anyways since everything's basically CAPUT, I'm opening up Tinder on my phone. A perfect logical substitution to the Paris nightlife.

Okay let's see, Emily— naaa she looks dry. I keep swiping and I'm just seeing bare girls that look as dry as her. Not everyday look like a bloody primary school teacher, not the vibes right now.

Just when dissatisfaction was hitting on how bleak the options are, Oxi messages me. *U in Paris rn? Ur location looks close to me atm, unless Tinder's just bugging.*

Nah it's not, I'm in Paris. I write back.

Let's link, she writes. *I'm in Paris with Jezza.*

Wow what are the odds of that, huh? Sure, I write. Something definitely smells off about the fact they're both here though. It just doesn't make sense why they'd be here.

How comes ur in Paris tho? I write.

We came for this rave, you should come— we picked up ;) She writes.

I look up at Mazzy whose halfway done with his zoot, "Do you wanna come to a rave tonight?"

"A rave? Mate everything's closed," he says putting down the zoot.

"Yeah, sure it'll probably be illegal but fun— come on. Life's gonna be such a bore with fucking Coronavirus who knows when we'll get another chance to go to a rave in Paris together? And to be honest, I'm fucking bored mate," I say.

"O.K. but where is it?" He asks.

"I don't know, lemme ask."

I'll come with my mate, send addy. I write.

It's been a while since Mazzy and I have been walking in the darkness, we've been following Google Maps to reach the address Oxi sent me earlier.

"So, whose this girl we're linking?"

"Oxi, glasses, blue hair— hot. Met her on Tinder the day I lost the bomb. And her friend, Jezza. Haven't got much of an opinion on him," I say.

"Oh, is that right? The night you lost the bomb? You decided to use Tinder then, didn't you that night," he laughs. "Jokes."

"Yeah, it is what it is."

I can feel a drum through my feet. Music.

"Elmo, I think we're here," Mazzy says. He points to the distance, there's purple and blue lights coming from a building near us.

"SOS PLEASE SOMEONE HELP ME!" We hear someone shout. That's Rihanna's song, we're probably here, huh?

Mazzy and I walk closer till we're at the entrance. There's people standing outside, chatting smoking, kissing. I walk inside, the masses of people inside sweating make the air inside feel a lot warmer than it was outside. There's no breeze.

Fuck, it's hot.

"Elmo!" I hear, I turn around and see Oxi. She's wearing a bra and a mini skirt with cowboy boots. She comes up to me and hugs me, pushing herself up against me. "I can't believe you're here," she says.

"I can't believe *you're* here," I counter.

She holds out her fingers that are pinching something small between them. She hovers her hand in front of my face, "Open." I open my mouth and she places the tab onto my tongue, inside.

I close my mouth, and let the paper dissolve in my saliva before I swallow the acid.

"So, is this Oxi, yeah?" Mazzy asks as he comes up behind me.

"Oxi, this is my mate, Mazzy—" I motion to her with my arm, "—Mazzy, Oxi."

"Nice to meet you, you from London?"

"Yeah, you too I hear… Elmo's always *Tindering* around, huh?" He says chuckling. The lights are flashing, and I wanna dance.

I start swaying, head's bopping, hips lowering. Oxi catches my drift and comes up on me. Then I see Mazzy doing the same with some random person. He's definitely not sober.

"What you on, Mazzy?" I shout over the music.

"I'm pinging," he shouts back, "Want some?"

"YESSS, GIMMEEE!" Oxi shouts.

"Wasn't talking to you, but sure— I got enough for you too babe," he says coming closer to us. Oxi holds out her hand and Mazzy places the pill in her palm.

Mazzy holds his closed fist in front of me, I open my tongue and he shoves it in there, fist and all. I clamp my mouth down on his wrist, locking him.

I can feel him dropping the pill down my throat.

He's looking at me and I'm looking at him, I know what he wants me to do and I have no choice.

My tongue swirls around his fist and he smirks.

Mazzy, O how I've missed you.

He pulls his hand out of my mouth and in comes his other with the open wine bottle.

SLURP.

Gag.

SLURP

Gag.

This time when he removes his hand from my mouth, it grabs my face hard and he's kissing me. I kiss him back, harder.

Oxi's grinding on me, harder.

She's active.

Mazzy turns to her and kisses her.

He's active.

It wasn't long before they were full on making out. I move myself from them and start swaying to the music. Full on techno was playing now.

THUD, THUD, THUD.

BOP, BOP, BOP.

My head was moving, arms swiping like cards in a card machine. You know it's not everyday contactless, even on the dance floor.

I start looking around at the sweaty bodies, no one's flexing here, everyone's too busy trying to get caught up in someone else's sexuality. Sometimes, just sometimes squat raves in London do it for me. Like I know they used to, considering Mazzy and I were always trekking from rave to rave.

Thinking back on it now, I do kinda miss those times, I look at him. He's still on Oxi locked in a long kiss. That's hot. The blue of her hair looks purple under the red lights, as his hands fist her hair. That's when I realise, the wine bottle on the floor, the red libation of their greeting pooling at their feet.

The birth of Venus, huh? More like the birth of fuckery on the dance floor.

They're moving closer together, I can barely see any space between them. Her body firmly presses against his, grinding, slowly. Then I see Oxi's face break away from his, her head throws back in a moan.

Trailing my eyes downward, Mazzy's hand has disappeared somewhere. One of Oxi's legs hikes up, and hooks around the back of his thigh.

The pleats of her skirt reveal his hand. I'm dead, it's like *that*, yeah Mazzy?

I'm still dancing, but the live porn be helping my high reach some kind of stable moment, where I can see everything slowly and— I mean everything. The blues, reds and purples all bursting into one around them — maybe it's the acid or maybe it's just me— but this is the best soft porn I've ever seen, and that's saying something because I've seen a lot.

There's an orange streak coming towards me from them, big but with thin swirls of red, dots of yellow twinkling-christmasy-tree lights joining the purple haze suddenly all around.

I look around and see some random with a flask, which reminds me— I'm hella thirsty right now. Not sure for what, but that'll do. I grab it from their loose hand, it basically just dropped into my paw. It was a like a swaying motion, everything's so slow and that random was so weak. Ha.

I'm pretty sure I'm laughing right now, not really sure why either but that's just life, init. I take a swig from the flask, which luckily had no lid. I don't know if I could hack dealing with unscrewing a cap right now.

I'm gulping more of this drink, it's lemonade and gin. Nice. I stole the right flask.

I'm fucking high right now, well what else do you expect at a fucking rave, huh? Sunshine, dandelions and rainbows? Well…

Shit…

I'm seeing a rainbow coming over the dancing sweaty bodies, with the colourful haze of explosive shapes coming from Mazzy and Oxi as a backdrop. Theres fucking flowers now too.

Fuck, maybe I shouldn't have had the acid *and* the pingers. I don't know if I'm still buzzing like a card in a card machine on the dance floor— all I know is that I'm vibing.

Here, *right now.*

I'm spinning. Everything's swirling around me like a transparent egg being whisked with lines of fucked up colour.

"Elmo!"

I'm sinning, round and round and round.

"ELMO!" I come to an abrupt stop. Hands are on me, anchoring me.

I blink a couple times, because I can't see who the fuck this is with all the colourful fogs. My vision, clearly, is still spinning around, flicking around like it's some sorta paint brush.

"ELMO!" Oh fuck, it's Jezza.

"What are you doing here?"

"Oxi told ya to come, nah? We came for this?"

"Oh, yeah shit I forgot," I reply. Jezza shakes his head, then starts looking around at the dancing people. They're the same people you see at most raves, although it's my first French one— I recognise the vibe.

A rave's a rave.

Nitty people will always clamour together at raves, who gives a fuck about if y'all speak the same language or not. No matter the city or country, where the crackheads are— that's home. So these lot coming here, for *this* seems lowkey kinda fucking stupid…

"What's so special about some rave in Paris— like you's could've gone to one in London you know," I start.

"Yeah, but like Oxi's mate organised this thing, and tonight's meant to be some sort of real special night," he explains.

"O.K."

"Where's Oxi? You seen her?"

I laugh, "Oh, I've *seen* her alright," he gives me a puzzled look.

"Where's she at then?"

I point to the space behind me, where the colour was still bursting from them, "There she is."

Jezza looks behind my head, "Naaa she's not." Well he's clearly on something too then because—

I turn my head around.

Blink. Okay lemme blink again.

Naaa it's not working, gotta rub my eyes. All I'm seeing is the colourful painting left behind Mazzy and Oxi getting it on. Minus them. Oh crap, I've lost Mazzy.

I turn to Jezza, "This always happens at raves mate— you lose people— but they always turn up after a while. Don't worry they'll be back somewhere—"

"—They?"

He looks confused, but I just remembered his delusion about being in love with Oxi, "AHHH, Oxi and Mazzy—"

"—Mazzy?"

"My mate Mazzy and her were... *getting to know each other*," Damn... I'm thinking back on that live porn, and I can't help but smirk.

"They— WHAT?"

For fuck's sake, can the dude not hear?

O, yeah shit, forgot. We're at a rave. A French one at that.

"THEY WERE GETTING TO KNOW EACH OTHER!"

He comes closer to me, "WHAT DO YOU MEAN?"

"Bruv," I begin looking down at him. He's bare close to me, I can feel his sweat. "THEY WERE 2 SECONDS AWAY FROM FUCKING ON THE BLOODY DANCE FLOOR."

"Oh," he says looking down. He looks so sad, but at the same time so stupid. The guy genuinely needs to face reality.

"How long you been in closet for?"

"Closet?"

"Bruv, you tell yourself you love Oxi or whatever, but you can't get it up— she's supposed to be the girl of your dreams."

"I was nervous, BECAUSE I'm in love with her mate," he says, a 'duh' look adopting his face straight after.

"Oh yeah? Then what was it she was saying? That day, about the fact that you couldn't get it up with this *other girl* you pulled?"

"I… er…"

"Exactly."

"I'm still into girls, though,"

"Oh yeah? Then how comes your body doesn't work with them?" He doesn't say anything. "I'm pretty sure the day the feds busted my flat, I had cum leaking from my arsehole. Doesn't take a genius to figure it was you."

"Me?"

"Yeah, you. Oxi doesn't have a dick, *trust me I know*."

"Yeah I know too."

"So, you admit you fucked me, yeah?"

"Yeah."

"Why'd you deny it?"

"Deny? I didn't deny it," he mumbles. Pussy.

"Bruv, you should count yourself lucky. I'm not one to be fucked, I like fucking till I drop, not the other way around. My sexy red self be too much for you, yeah? Your animal instincts kicked in with all my furry red goodness, yeah?"

"I wouldn't say goodness, more like softness," he says. "Was I your first?"

"Nah, of course not. But not gonna lie— it's not gonna happen again— I must've been *so* out of mind that I still don't remember shit about that night."

"Yeah we were all really fucked that night." He's still so close to me that can feel his pants buzzing against me. I look down and don't see his hard piece, instead it's his phone screen lighting up inside his jean pocket.

"Yo, you gonna get that?"

"Get what?"

"Bruv, how high are you? Your phone, mate." With that he digs up his phone. Looks like it's stopped ringing, but I wouldn't know anyway I feel like all I can hear is this conversation because the music just blares out everything else.

"It's Oxi, she and your mate left. They're outside on a street corner waiting for the Uber, it comes in twenty though because we're in the middle of nowhere right now. She text me a location pin. Let's go."

Jezza starts walking out in front of me, the masses of people still everywhere. Shit, I'm gonna lose him.

Fuck.

I can't see his head anymore.

I stand still and look around for him. Nope, nada.

"ELMO!" Oh, suddenly he appears out of nowhere and grabs my red paw.

It took a while for us to get to the location Oxi sent Jezza. A load of twisting, turning and stumbling in the dark but we made it, just barely. We had to sprint for the last five. But we made it.

Oxi and Mazzy are sat in the back with me and Jezza's in the front with the driver. These two keep giving each other looks the whole way. I don't even know where we're going, but at this point I'm just enjoying the buzz of my high.

I'm looking out the window watching the streets of Paris pass us by. Mazzy and Oxi are snogging next to me, some random French radio is playing in the background. It wasn't long before we got out and started heading up some stairs.

Oxi knocks on the door and an older woman opens the door, "Mon ami." She says and hugs Oxi. She introduces all of us and the woman, who Oxi said was called Cynthia, ushers us in. The apartment is dimly lit, and voices hit me. Some sorta smooth French vinyl music is playing in the room.

I look around, hot French people. Love that. Of course, in Paris the so-called city of love and haven for fashion— everyone's peng.

Cynthia though, she's really hot. I'm just watching her talk to Mazzy and Oxi. Don't know where Jezza's gone— but I couldn't care less to be honest.

I sit down on the sofa, there's some other people sat around it having their own conversations in French, but smoking. I need a fucking blem right about now.

"Can I have a blem?" I ask. The people stop talking and look at me, confused. "A cigarette?" Maybe this they'll understand.

"Ahh, of course—" a girl says, taking the box of straights from her lap and leaning over the side to hand it to me.

I put it in my mouth and realise I need a light. I'm patting myself down when I feel it spark. I look up and it's Cynthia who's lit it. She's in my complete vision, taking up everything. Her long brown hair, and black tight dress. She lights her own straight, while her eyes are on mine, and blows the first puff in my direction. It's like I'm a pigeon and she's the Eiffel tower, the way she's standing so tall and I'm sat down on the sofa. Older woman though, you gotta love them. They'll lived life, you get me— that's hot.

She sits down on the armrest of the sofa, right next to me.

Inhale.

"So, Elmo is it?" The way she says that with her French accent is fucking sexy and she knows that. Damn. The way she's looking at me I feel like a year 7 being too shook to walk past the year 9's chilling outside the entrance of McDonald's. She's stripping me down with those eyes.

Exhale.

Oh boy am I in trouble…

Inhale.

"Ummm Hmmm…" I say.

"Cat got your tongue, Elmo?" She laughs, and smokes more of her straight. I'm already halfway down through mine. Shit. She's only just started. "So what do you do?"

What do I do? "I don't know to be honest…"

"*Really?*" She says in an exaggerated manner. She thinks I'm joking. I legit don't even know what the bloody hell *I* do.

I… I know have *a* life.

Something I…

Something I did… but I just can't seem to remember at this point.

Fuck, I'm way too high to be using my brain for hard questions right now. Let's shut her up. I grab her face and give her a long kiss. She breaks it for a smoke, and I take the chance to finish mine and dash it somewhere.

She straddles me and we just kiss. The music's changed and I can hear bare sound right now. Seems like people are fucked right now. We're still snogging on the sofa. I start to unzip the back of her dress, she lets the straps fall down. I grab a big fistful of her breasts squeeze them.

My red furry fella gets up.

He's active.

The snog breaks and she adjusts herself onto him, then sinks down.

She moans.

She smokes and sinks down again on me, slowly. This feels good. My eyes close. Nothing can beat this feeling.

S.E.X.

Damn, it's been way TOO long.

Louder moans.

OooH, OuuuuH.

SLAP. FAP. SLAP.

I open my eyes because I know Cynthia ain't making those sounds. She's smoking. I look around at the room, and there's clothes everywhere. Mazzy and Oxi are fucking, naked. Mazzy's pounding into her, she's snogging some random girl and Jezza… Jezza's wanking, naked while watching.

What did I say? Best live porn.

Am I right or am I right?

Cynthia follows my eyes, and looks back. Her face turns back to me with a smirk. She gets off me and gets on the floor. Her face is facing me, as she starts crawling backwards towards Mazzy and Oxi. I get down on all fours and follow her lead.

Her wish is my command. Respect your elders and all that.

She stops, so I stop. She launches herself forward at me, grabbing a fistful of my red furs and kisses me, hard. Then she pushes me back and starts giving me head.

I close my eyes and moan.

My mouth suddenly feels wet.

I don't know whose, but there's a vagina in my face. I know it's not Cynthia because she's still giving me head. But who cares, the only thing to do in this situation is eat. So I do.

Moans just fill the room from all corners. What is this? A sex house? I don't care and I don't know. I fucking love it.

I love the fucking French.

Cynthia's head is starting to become really sloppy, but I just can't move right now. I can't even ask wagwan. I'm licking a pussy out right now. Fuck, fuck, fuck. Not sure if I'm fucked or just like… fuck. You know, like damn…

Fuck.

PLOP.

My dick slides out of Cynthia's mouth like a lollipop to make way for her moans and groans. She's either struggling to breathe or someone's giving it to her fucking good.

A hand comes to my dick and starts sliding it up and down. They're wanking me off. Then there's another wet lick, before someone starts sliding a rubber down.

Jeeze, who is this? It's a bit late for a condom now, mate.

Suddenly someone is sinking down, and fuck it's bloody tight. This is why you don't slide on shitty Johnny's. Oh well, not my problem.

AHHHH.

It's Jezza. I start laughing, clearly no sound is coming out; but the person I'm eating starts squirming the more I laugh. I lick more and more, the cum is DRIPPING.

Moans.

The pussy lifts off my face, and I look up— it's the girl that gave me a straight earlier. I look around the room to see what the fuck is going on, because clearly, there's a lot. There's some random French dude that I remember talking to Miss. Cigarette & eat my pussy currently using me as a dildo.

Eh, it's not like I mind— that's life, init? We all got needs. Man saw an opportunity and took it.

Mazzy's fucking Cynthia, and Oxi's got her legs wide open facing Jezza and Cynthia's fingering her.

Oh and Jezza— I don't know what round he's on with himself over there— but he's moaning the loudest out of everyone.

Fuck, man. I can't believe he fucked me. Naaa, nope. It didn't happen.

This guy has got live, interactive porn—a fucking foursome going on, and he's just sitting there wanking as if he wasn't in the same bloody room as us.

What a bloody wet-wipe wanker.

ELEVEN

I'm sitting in the car waiting for Mazzy to get out of Richard's. It's already that time, can you believe it? I can't. Last night was just this never ending saga. I still feel fucking high. I bloody love it though, just wish we hadn't left Cynthia's sex house— but alas things must come to an end. They always do, sooner or later. Nothing's forever.

It's not long before I see Mazzy walking out of the front door. He gets in and sighs.

"Mate, we need to get back asap. Boris announced London's going into lockdown."

"What? Are you serious?"

"Yup. He actually did it."

"Wow. So man actually cares, yeah?"

"Naaa, I don't think so. Man was shamed into it. Have you not heard about Italy bruv. Just look at Paris mate."

"Well… Let's just get out of here."

"Yeah, you're right—" he dumps a black duffel bag onto my lap, "—here."

I open the bag and peak inside, it's a new bomb-looking thing. Great. Just great. *Wooohooo, bomb time.*

We start driving through the streets of Paris. They're deserted, just like how they were when we arrived. You'd think people would be out though, it's hot. Every time it's hot in London people pile onto the streets—obligations or not. They're like the sun's out, bun's out. Bruv, it's like *everyone.* I wouldn't be surprised if parents would fully allow their kids to call in sick from school just so they can appreciate the bloody sun.

Lockdown though, kinda unbelievable. Like Macron cares about his people and whatnot well, I like to think so… in comparison to bloody fucking Boris, man. That guy needs to go, bruv. If I can help that happen, I'm game. If the guy's not gonna resign, man's gotta give man a nudge into oblivion. Not the, oooh I'm in some ET type-shit but the, oh fuck Imma die type-shit.

I'm looking over at Mazzy. He's actually really hot, like I'm surprised he isn't seeing someone. Although, it's not like I've asked, I'm just assuming that because he hasn't talked about anyone to me nor introduced me to someone.

"Maz, you seeing anyone right now?"

"What do you mean, mate? I'm seeing you."

Huh? The fuck does that mean?

"You taking the piss, right now?"

"Naaa, I'm serious." He says, looking at the road.

"Errrr…"

Like I know we kinda, sorta used to have a thing, but I got bad vibes from Mazzy recently. We definitely, one hundred percent aren't as close we used to be so…

Even getting here, to fucking France was a struggle. Man nearly left me, abandoned on the bloody motorway for fuck's sake.

Seeing me? Piss off.

I don't even 'see' me. I'm looking at man in disbelief. Is man serious?

He's looking at me now, straight in the eyes. He looks serious.

Oh no. Ooooh no, OOOOOOOOH NOOOOOO.

Silence.

Na, NOPE.

Silence.

Guy's gone mad.

Silence. Followed by more silence, all we can hear is the wheels of the car going over some French cobbled road because I'm not saying anything and neither is he. He's just looking at me and I'm just looking at him, too.

VROOOM. Buuuuump. VROOOM.

"Elmo, I'm fucking with you. You think, I think *THIS* is a relationship? *Mad.* That's fucking mad. *I'm not INSANE*," he laughs. He lightly starts slapping the steering wheel in his laughter.

Well, thank fuck for that. It's a joke.

"That *would be insane*."

"Yup. C-R-A-Z-Y," he laughs, dryly. Why do I sense some kinda awkwardness from him though? That doesn't make sense… It's a joke.

He's joking… right?

I don't even *wanna* think about Mazzy's bad joke not being a joke… That's a can of worms I don't have time for. Some other day, but not right now when I'm in his fucking car holding a fucking bomb. Not the time.

"You never answered the question though," I point out. Man thinks I'm stupid. Well he's got a reason. Most people just assume I'm some stupid, sexy, horny red furry shit.

"What was the question?"

"Are you seeing someone?"

"I'm always seeing someone, Elmo. You know that," he says.

"Well, no. Not really. It's not like you've talked to me about anyone. I thought you were going through some sorta dry patch. I was even glad you got with Oxi, like for once— you're getting some you know. Putting yourself to good use."

"Good use?" He laughs. "You're funny. Just cause I don't chat about what I do, and who I do, don't mean I don't do, you get me?"

The recent people I don't / won't probably ever chat about, sandpit girl and Apollo. So… yeah, okay— I'll give him that. We all have shit we don't talk about. Guess we just don't talk anymore. What do I expect though? I don't even pick up the phone…. Well, that's just because I know it's always got something to do with what I've *gotta* do. Which most of the time, I don't *wanna* do.

I really, honestly can't even pinpoint when I just starting knowing he wasn't calling me for a catch up. I don't even remember when the last time was that I called him for something other *than* a pick up.

Damn, when your friends turn into your dealers, you really do lose something. I didn't lose my drugs, but I lost my mate.

Shit then, that got deep. Good thing he can't read minds. I wonder when he noticed though? When did I just become a shot to him? I still remember when we used to do whatever *that* was back then.

We never even got to the bottom of that, but that's probably why we're still friends, *if* we even still are. Man, life's fucking confusing. Nothing's ever just black and white is it? There's always gotta be *Fifty fucking Shades of Grey*.

The engine turns off. We've stopped. Mazzy stopped the car. Are we already at the ferry port? Can't be. I look around, we're in some French field. Nothing but green grass and trees. This ain't no port.

"Why'd you stop?" I ask.

"I— "

"—You what?" I cut in, this is annoying. When the bloody hell are we gonna get back if man is randomly stopping in random-as-fuck places? Man's lost his marbles, bruv.

"I thought it'd be nice to chill for a bit. Talk." He says.

"*Talk?*" Man's not serious.

"Yeah. Talk."

"Talk about what?"

"Well, clearly there's stuff we gotta air out. Like…"

"Like…?"

"This is what I mean we gotta… *talk*." Man's actually serious.

"OK."

Well whatever this is about, he's piqued my interest. I chuck the duffel bag in the feet compartment before getting out of the car. I sit on the hood of the car, Mazzy's standing in front of me.

He's just looking at me. There's no words. Where's his words, huh? He's the one that stopped the car and wanted to 'talk'.

"You gonna say something then? Because I don't think Boris is gonna wait till we're back before putting London on Lockdown. We don't have time for this."

"Oh, so now that *I* wanna talk, all of a sudden you wanna make it in time for lockdown, yeah?"

"Well I'd rather not be locked out of my own country, thank you very much."

"I don't think it works like that."

"Well, how'd you know it doesn't?"

"Urm... well, I don't."

"Exactly. So, let's fucking get on with it then, wagwan with you?"

"You can be such a dick sometimes, Elmo." I give him a duh look.

"I never pretended to be otherwise. I've always been a prick."

"I hate you." He says.

"*Oh, yeah?*" I laugh. "That's not news."

"I love you."

"*Sure.*"

"Fuck. You. Elmo." He spits. What a feisty boy, what's got his knickers in a twist?

"Alright, *fuck me.*"

"*What?*"

"I said alright. You wanna fuck me, fuck me. *I don't care.*"

"You don't care? YOU DON'T CARE?!"

"Na, not really."

"I'll give you something to care about then," he says. He takes a quick stride to me.

Suddenly, he's all up in face. Then he kisses me hard.

BANG.

He's pushing me down hard, onto the cold metal of his car. He's gripping me everywhere, but I don't care, still. What's he getting at? He's gonna make me care? Idiot. Just because I'm kissing him back don't mean shit. His hands are running up and down my sides.

I can feel him, he's as hard as the metal behind my back. He's hotter, though. In all senses of the word. He's kissing me all over now. I'm still laying back, I'm not gonna do anything. This is all on him. He's the one at it.

OUCH. He just pinched my thigh. Am I bleeding? *That fucker.*

Nope, nope. I don't care.

"How long you gonna do this for?"

"I thought you said you don't care?" He asks, pinching me some more. I don't know what the hell he's doing right now. I can't tell if he's playing some joke or being stupid at this point. He's acting like a kid throwing a tantrum because he didn't get what he wanted. And just like some kid pulling and tugging at their parents pants' trying to embarrass them into submission, he's tugging at me. It's not gonna work on me though, he should know I have no shame.

Man needs to grow up. He's trying to teach me some sort of lesson right now, but I think he's the one that will leave with one instead. He *knows* me. So… he should know better. That whatever this is, isn't going to work.

He's on top of me, and raises himself up like he's doing a push up, looking down at me. He doesn't look right. He doesn't look like Mazzy right now. I'm not crazy. I know it's him. It smells like him, I know it's him… but something about the way he's watching me right now… I don't think he's looked at me like this before.

Or maybe… He's kinda like…

Is it just me or was he moving with this same energy when he kicked me out of the car onto the motorway yesterday? When he just exploded about how I was a shit friend.

Ah, fuck.

I don't wanna think about all this, so I close my eyes. Out of sight, out of mind. Lemme find some godforsaken peace of mind.

I'm feeling his tongue on me, licking me like some panting dog, up and down. Breathing heavy all up on me. His bitterness is all over, this little play of his is kinda insane. But I kinda like it.

I'm just pushing back, like I'm in the backseat, a passenger being taken for a ride. Damn, I'm really something, Mazzy's tryna scare me here, clearly. Yet what can I do? Can't help it if it's not working.

He's literally doing *nothing*.

BANG.

He's grabbed my wrists and pinned them above my head, then slammed them into the glass behind me. Hmm, pain. *Nice.*

More. Gimme more, Mazzy. "Come on, that's all you got?"

"You want more?"

"Make me bleed." I say, Mazzy looks over at me real quick before averting his eyes down me like a snake slithering down a ladder. He grabs my dick. I'm surprised I'm hard. I didn't even realise.

He squeezes hard in the middle. It's lowkey kinda painful, kinda feel like I wanna pee but at the same time I don't. I know it's not cum.

AHHHH. Fuck.

Mazzy's pushed the head of his dick into me. He's stuck. Fuck. This hurts like a bitch.

FUCK, FUCK— I think one of his hands are grabbing onto the windshields behind me, using them to ground himself and exert more force. More pain. I try to move my paws but there's still a grip on them.

He's serious. He's actually gonna give me more, "FUCCCCCCCK".

He's penetrated me, his dick pushes through me. Fuck, fuck, fuck. This hurts sooo much, I can feel rips everywhere. Like all the seams of my furry flesh flooding out. Red, definitely red.

As soon as he starts moving, I let out a scream. I can't help it, this is fucking tearing me apart. I'm trying to move my hands, but his grip isn't budging. Fuck. I don't want to scream.

I clamp my mouth shut.

He pounds me again.

"HaaaH… Arghh…. HNNNGH."

And again.

I jolt to life. I can't stop my mouth anymore. My lips won't stay shut.

"ARGGGGGH….haaa….ARGGGHHH….haaa … NGH".

He thrusts again.

SQUELCH. What's this? It's my cum. I'm dripping.

Pound. PoUND. POUND.

I'm screaming at this point.

He just penetrates harder, faster.

I scream so loud, I'm pretty sure the stars above our heads are awake. I can feel my paws trembling. Actually trembling.

As he keeps going, I'm staring to feel myself twitching, tickling deep inside.

"Uwahhh. Haaaaa…. Haaaa…." I can't cum again.

No… it's…

Too.

Much.

THRUSSST.

I flinch. My body just flinched by itself. Yet Mazzy's grip on me is hard. It didn't do a thing.

He continues. At this point, I'm moaning all over the place like some bitch. It feels good.

I lay my head back on the car and look up at Mazzy's face expecting to see some beast-like expression but to my surprise that isn't what I find.

He's crying. *Mazzy's crying.*

SHOVE.

If he's so mad at me…

SQUELCH.

Why does he look so sad?

SHOVE.

I'm the one bleeding…

SQUELCH.

But why is he the one crying?

DRIIIIP.

Yet, worst of all… why does the small cascade of salty water dripping onto me feel like he's burning into me, and bleeding away into nothing?

Badum… BADUM… BAADUUUM.

TWELVE

Today's the day. The day that all that France trek was even about in the first place. The day I pay back my debt and get these motherfuckers I met through Mazzy off my back. Although, because I know Dyer's probably watching me somewhere, somehow... Like I gotta think like this now, considering I agreed to become the geezer's snitch, init. *Shit.* I'm not really sure this is gonna *really* be over now, is it? But we'll see, init.

Here's to hoping.

Normally for a day like today, you'd think Mazzy would've at least called me, or something you know. But nah, all I got was a text on the trap phone with a time and place.

Ever since that French field fuckery with Mazzy, I can tell he's been off with me. Considering last time I was moving around with a bomb in Heathrow airport he was on the phone with me, he was *there* every step of the way.

The last week since we've been back, I've heard absolutely zilch. That is until today, via the trap phone I keep in the tin bread box I copped from IKEA, God knows when.

When we finished our fuckery that day, he got up and into the car. While I was just laying there under the night's darkness, feeling like fucking death on the car hood.

Even I was surprised at how cold man was, he started driving. Actually driving off, with me still laying on the car hood. It got to a point I tried to sit up when he was going slow through the fields, but my arse hurt *waaaaay* too much. So I just clung onto the car hood the whole way into England.

Like it was dark, init. When we were on the ferry, I just slept with the car. I think Mazzy got off and did— whatever. Point is, we didn't say or utter a word to each other. I didn't wanna breach the subject of whatever the hell was going on with him. Nor did I wanna ask him wagwan with him, because last time I did that... whatever the heck that French field fuckery was, happened.

Mazzy though, I think he thought he'd said enough. I told him before his little lesson wouldn't work. I knew he'd be the one learning something instead, and I was fucking right, huh?

I don't know where Mazzy's head's at though. No matter how much I've wracked my brain about it this last week. Every time I think back to it, I'm just kinda lost for words. Like I think he hates me, right?

But no matter, who I've fucked this week, and been fucked by... I can't get those tears out of my head. I don't know why, but every time I remember how painfully they burned me, I start twisting inside...

In ways I don't wanna know...

I don't know... I don't fucking know what's wrong with me.

I took some train to get here, satchel in tow. Before I left I took the bomb out of the duffel bag (the one Mazzy and I got from Richard that night) and put it into one of my many leather bags so I can swig it over me. Plus, it's so cliché, a bomb in a black duffel bag. I don't even remember if it was a Nike or Adidas one— it's probably one of the two anyways.

I'm walking down the road, all I'm seeing is fancy little English houses— the kind that belong in the countryside, you get me. Well it's not hard to believe this because I'm in Oxfordshire. But even in London though, there's bare places like this all around the city. I don't need to look at my trusty friend, Google Maps to find where I'm supposed to be.

I can see it right ahead. The flock of reporters and camera's clicking and flicking off outside this one yard is a dead giveaway. X marks the spot, and all that.

As I get closer I see what the flocks are gathered around. The Prime Minister with a spaghetti bird's nest for hair. Boris Johnson, out on the lawn in a scruffy jumper with some next-up sport-type logo on it. He's holding a tray with mugs and a carton of milk.

"Would you comment?" A reporter asks, pointing the microphone at him. Her camera man behind her, shoving his equipment in his direction.

"W-Would you like a cup of tea?" Boris responds, holding the tray to her. Then sort of wobbling around her and her people— away from the mic.

"Yeah, sure. Thank you, thank you," she says shoving her mic in front of him again. "Do you regret —"

"—Would you like a cup of tea?"

"Do you regret that thousands of people have —"

"—Would you like a cup of tea?" He interrupts again shoving the tray around the swarm of press people.

"I'll have one," some guy says.

Boris holds the tray up for the guy to grab a mug, like a *fucking* mug *for* the fucking mug. I can't believe this guy is falling for Boris' press distraction. I'll bet his boss isn't gonna be too happy to see the guy he sent out to get a scoop on the PM, ironically getting scooped up instead by Boris and his *fucking* tea. Good luck keeping that job come Monday morning, mate. "Have a cup of tea," the reporter takes the tea, "There you go."

The female reporter gets up in Boris' grill again, "Do you regret your decisions as Prime Minister? People have died because of you—"

"—I—I want you to have a cup of tea—"

"—If I have a cup of tea are you going to answer my questions?—"

"—No, I—I'm solely on a humanitarian mission… you've been here all day and you've been *incredibly* patient and I feel very sorry for you—"

I'd love to make *a patient* out of him, a hospital one that is. Prick. He's a prick, definitely more than me, one hundred percent.

"—Do you feel sorry for the families of the people you *sacrificed* with your dishonesty?—"

"—H-Have some tea." He finishes for her, "I've got nothing to offer you except some tea, okay?" It really seems like this is going nowhere. I see the death of British journalism right there, when she grabs a mug of tea.

"You got any biscuits?" She asks, while sipping some tea. Wow. Just wow. The man is an imbecile, yet this whole cuppa charade really fucking works, huh? Is he a political genius or just plain stupid? I guess we'll never know, but times like this really makes me think sometimes.

Boris is pretending. He's tryna convince us all that he's this clown, when really he's something else— what that is— I got no clue. It's all smoke and mirrors.

Bruv, my head hurts just thinking about this— and I've got a job to do.

I walk away from the swarm of press. I don't want to draw attention— there's people—loads of people and camera's— lot's. This bad.

Is Mazzy crazy? Yeah, sure I've got balls but bruv— I'm not exactly the type that *doesn't* draw attention. I'm big, red and furry. Man's stupid. I'm looking around though, it makes sense why he sent me here. There's no security, and by the looks of it Boris is caught off guard seeing as he looks like he's in PJ's. This was clever, if this was Downing Street there's no way I would've gotten this close.

It's lowkey invading man's privacy but you kinda lose that when you're running the bloody country. So boo-hoo I don't feel sorry for him, sorry— no, not sorry.

How Mazzy even knew the PM wasn't in London though, but here beats me. How Mazzy even knew I'd be able to come here because reporters were moving mad on his lawn, is also a fucking mystery. Bruv, does he have a guy on the inside? In the media maybe or somewhere in politics?

Not gonna lie though, I can't imagine Mazzy rubbing shoulders with them sort of people, you get me. People with a stick up their fucking arseholes, although he'd get on with people that speak their mind like that female reporter, but then her lack of backbone would send him FLYING to ghost her *the fuck* outta his life. Although… if any of them needed a dealer for some gear, he's your guy— so maybe he's their guy too. You'd be surprised how easily getting high transcends rational, getting-to-know-and-understand-you barriers between people. Look no further than how me meeting Oxi and subsequently Jezza has escalated. None of us really know jack-shit about each other, and that's O.K.

That's just how it be, you get me.

I'm starting to take in the house. It's huge, but I wanna avoid reporters and that— obviously. Behind Boris there's his *what I'm assuming* car is, on his driveway leading to most likely… some sort of garden that you can't see fully from the street. His neighbours would have easy access though, wouldn't they….?

I make a U-turn and walk away, away from the crowd— enough that they won't be (hopefully) looking in my direction. The worst case scenario is that one of these camera-birds ends up recording me. Now THAT would be TV gold. Imagine, red furry monster blows up BoJo…

I'm wheezing… but nope.

No— can't laugh out loud right here. I DON'T laugh quietly— If I open my mouth, I just know all them eyes that should be inspecting what our Prime Minister is doing with his tea and biscuits would be on me instead.

So I don't laugh.

I look at the neighbour's house and make a bee-line for it. I'm actually just jogging but I feel like a champ— can't help it. It's been a while since I ran, not gonna lie. Can't even believe these legs of mine are even fucking working.

When's the last time I fed them? Fed them?

Shit.

What about my mouth?

Well… Alcohol has calories in it, right? Wine's made from grapes— that's one of my five a day then, wow look at that.

ME, Elmo living that health conscious life…

Pfftt, yeah right.

I'm at the house next door, and would you look at that… I can't hear a thing, not a peep. Meaning, no one's home init. *Marvellous.*

I stroll past the side of the front, that was kinda identical to Boris' place. I'm passing the side of the house, and I keep going till I'm in their garden area. Wow. Can't believe this idea of mine worked. Mazzy would be proud.

Shit.

Why'd I mention him… *I love to kill my own mood, huh?*

I would love a blem right about now but it's not the time.

I haven't even gotten to Boris' place yet and I know myself. I can't screw this would up, imagine. I could blow myself up and that's not happening. Well… I hope not.

I just wanna get this over and done with, ever since we got back from France I've had this thing sitting inside the fridge in my shit flat. I'm not really sure that's where you're meant to store a bomb, but like— it didn't exactly come with a manual, you get me. Mazzy's advice last time got it lost, remember? And that couldn't let that happen to this one, especially since we had to trek to France for this thing.

I don't think you can understand the stress of having a bomb just sitting in your yard. Like you go to the park and look at birds and nonces and only you know there's a fucking bomb in your yard… Like come on, when the fuck did my life turn into this mess?

Like seriously, I'm just your regular-mesgular crackhead, like there's no need to add domestic terrorist to that, you get me? It's not like I wanna do this, you know. But it's like, if I don't— I die.

So… it doesn't leave me much choice now, does it?

It's always the mules at the bottom of the food chain that gotta be blackmailed or whatever, into doing whatever they gotta do—

Like who am I to judge you know, life is life. My life may not be a fairytale, not some picture perfect balance of what a man should be, but it's mine… But while I've got *this* hanging over my head, anything I do… everything I say, eat— whatever… it doesn't feel like it's me.

Like it's *mine*.

So many people trying to own me, and it feels like I'm somebody else. I don't wanna be overwhelmed, and I don't wanna have someone else's hands hovering me; over my vessels and sending signals to my nervous system, moving them. I WANT TO. I WANT TO MOVE MYSELF.

While I still have this fucking bomb— I'm not myself. I'm not some warrior for whatever, I'm not some brainwashed idiot. I'm not some crazy fanatic. I'm just your regular red furry guy. I'm just tryna live my fucking life.

At this point it's more like, two birds one stone you know. I do this job, that's it and if I'm being honest Boris Johnson isn't at the top my Christmas list… Not sure he's on anyone's Christmas list. Bruv if I was Santa, he'd be barred forever to be on the naughty list. Not like that sort of shit is even real though.

Although I'd probably definitely be on the naughty list, right next to Boris, huh? The irony.

Like I'm no saint. I know that. I hurt people and I like it. Does that make me sick? Like some kinda sicko…? Maybe… Naaa, it probably does. Maybe if I've got time I'll pop by my GP and see if they can see what's wrong with me.

Although… I'm not sure I know *how* to be anything but what I am right now.

I'm not even sure I'll ever *want* to be anything than what I am right now.

This… is… too… much… thinking. I need to stop this shit, my life is on the line. I have a job to do. I can think later.

I need to wake THE FUCK up.

So…

I SLAP myself.

That wasn't HARD enough.

So…

I SLAP myself again HARDER.

And again, and again and again.

I'm looking at the brick wall I've gotta climb over. If logic exists, Boris' garden should be on the other side. I grab my balls and give them a squeeze.

Fuck. What am I? A pussy?

Some bitch…

Well…

Mazzy did… no… NOPE.

I'm doing this. *Fuck.*

When THE FUCK did I turn into this messy can of baked beans, bruv? I've got to get it together. Garden. Bomb. Boris. Out. Home. Life. Yes, that's it.

I grip the top of the wall and pull myself up. Low-key hard, if I'm being honest. Had to sort of push myself half up by stepping on a couple plant pots, but they were the grip I needed, init. They don't mind either, they're doing their public service duty. As Boris told that reporter, it's their 'humanitarian mission' init, so they're helping me get the bastard.

Bastard.

That bastard probably has a lot of them, we all know about that one from the affair like over a decade ago, but… like bruv. I don't know what it it about that frazzled sack of yellow head lice but he's apparently irresistible to some women, huh? Isn't he shacked up right now with some blonde young thing?

Oh well. That's just life, init.

Fuck's a fuck.

I don't know about much else, deep stuff and that. Not my thing. Go ask Jeremy Kyle init, he's the one that left his wife for his kid's babysitter.

Oh, now *that* was a great meme. Shame the show got cancelled. Jeremy Kyle memes were A*, some of them should really be illegal. Oh man, I'm remembering that meme where them gay dudes that were about to get married went on. They'd heard a rumour they were related, but wanted to check they weren't before they got married, and they'd been together for like 7 years or something.

Like, imagine your dating someone and people are saying you lot are related, kinda—maybe? That's just tapped. It's not like I'd know about dating anyone, but I can't imagine life's good if you're fucking your brother or sister, you get me?

Anyways, long story short turns out the dudes were related. Well they were half brothers, but pretty sure that was the end of their erm... sexual... romantic relationship, init? Must've been... *kinda* hard though, suddenly your fiancé is your half sibling. Which means no more fucking, that's for sure.

Hopefully. I hope they kept a lid on that after the show. Jesus— imagine if they didn't.

I'm shuddering. Let's stop thinking about this nonsense.

I look down from atop the wall, I can faintly hear stuff from the driveway where Boris is at with the press. This is the right one. Good. I've finally done something smart. I leap down, I don't land on my feet. I ain't some cat.

I get up from the floor and take a look around the garden. It's big and it's green, grass everywhere. Low-key overgrown in some places, obviously hasn't been tended to in a while but the little wild flowers here and there is pretty.

Honestly, not what I expected, not gonna lie. You'd think the Prime Minister's garden would be this peng picture perfect place. I guess his garden is as much of a mess as him. It still the baffles the complete fuck out of me, how this buffoon actually got voted in during the referendum…

Then again, Jeremy Corbyn wasn't exactly Jon Snow coming to save us all from winter and the Night Walkers, you get me?

I look at the garden table and chairs, there's papers on them and a black leather case with a cuppa. Either Boris was sitting here before he got caught up in the press or someone else is here. Crap if it's actually the later I've got to move quick.

Shit. Where should I put the bomb? Inside the house? In his car?

Can't do the car, because Boris and the press would see me, the car is in the driveway, where the swarm is. Fuck. House it is.

I go to the back door, it's glass and I can see through the conservatory I'm assuming, kind of like a sitting area. Rich people.

I open the door. It's unlocked. Of course its unlocked, the countryside life, huh? If this was London, man would've been robbed time ago. It's his lucky day today, he's in for a treat. Man's getting bombed today. Bet Boris never thought someone would do this. The man is stupid. He should've stayed in Downing Street. Anyhoo, ain't my issue.

A lot of people want him dead. Remember when some normal, kind-looking old lady said to some BBC person, "Don't you even mention that name in front of me, that *FLITHY piece of toe rag,*" and walked off from the camera when the BBC person started talking about Boris.

Damn, this job is for me to get my life back. But it'd be doing a lot of people a massive favour. So let me get back to it and stop procrastinating.

I take a step inside and just listen. I don't hear anything so I've got time. Not a lot but a little. Lemme put this bomb somewhere quick and get the fuck out of here.

I'm looking around for clues, how the heck am I meant to know where Boris chills in his yard? The kitchen? Naaa, the guy don't cook. He's in a love affair with Uber Eats. The toilet? Everyone uses the toilet, right? But I don't know where the toilet is though.

Shit.

Maybe, my dude'g gotta have an office here somewhere. Of course he's gotta have one, he's the Prime Minister. It'd be stupid if he didn't have one. But where's that? Fuck, Mazzy really should've given me some sort of instructions or something. Man just fully gave me a bomb and left it all up to me, huh? Really isn't like him, but then again I guess Maz didn't really wanna talk to me after all that French field fuckery but, bruv. This is important, isn't it?

Jeeze. Childish. Well… I—

—Not the time to think about nonsense. I've gotta plant this bomb somewhere.

Plant…

A plant?

Should I put it in a plant? Is there even a plant inside here? I'm looking around, there's a sofa kinda thing by the windows overlooking a bit of the garden. There's a denim jacket draped over the arm bit… and there's A PLANT! It's peaking up behind the corner of the sofa. Kinda tall. Probably has a big pot then.

Should I put it in the plant though? What if Boris doesn't come over here by the time it goes off?

Shit, it's a risk.

But I don't wanna risk moving about this house too much. I just wanna get the fuck out of here—

without fucking up my life. If I wanted to die, I'd just do what kamikaze's did, init and BAM.

But… I wanna fuck some more, drink some more and smoke some more too.

So, no.

I'm not gonna commit suicide on the account of Boris Johnson. He's not worth *that* much.

Fuck it.

Imma put this thing in the plant. If it gets him, it's gets him. If not, God bless my soul— because if he's not dead, I'm dead.

I walk over to the sofa, and push aside the jacket a bit so I can get a clearer view of the plant. Not gonna lie, I can't picture Boris in a denim jacket but I guess that's what's behind closed doors, init. I reach down and gently start trying to dig out the base of it from the soil.

What? I don't wanna make a mess, because then I'd have to clean it up. I know when the bomb goes off there will definitely be a big mess but logic you know. Common sense, I don't want anything to look out of place. Or else he might realise something's up and I can't have that.

I open my satchel and take out the bomb using one paw, the other is holding the plant I dug out. I put the bomb in the pot. I feel like there's something I should be pressing to turn it on. I know I'll detonate it remotely but I need to do something. Fuck where's Mazzy when you need him?

Fuck it, there's a red button connected to the screen of a trap phone that's connected with wires to the phone. I press the red button. The screen lights up. The Nokia logo comes up, then it a message appears on the screen.

Call me, to detonate. Yeah I know that. A number comes up on the screen. I didn't know the bomb's number. I whip out the trap phone Mazzy gave me— yes I brought it with me. I thought Mazzy would probably contact me, but it's coming in handy right about now.

I punch in the number and save it as Homerton b. I didn't wanna save it as just, bomb. Gotta give it some character, my guy won't be alive long. I hope he made some friends in my fridge and said his prayers. My little lamb, get ready for your slaughter.

Okay, that's done. That was easy. I put the plant on top of it and shift some of the soil around. I wouldn't know there was something else in there that wasn't meant to be. Shit, I did a good job.

Now, lemme get the fuck out of here. Finally. A much deserved blem is waiting for me when I get off this property. Like for real.

I shift the denim jacket back to where it was, slightly cover the plant and get out. I'm walking to the wall.

"Elmo?" What. The. Fuck. I turn around and see that wet-wipe wanker from Weatherspoons, Apollo.

"What the fuck are *you* doing here?" I ask.

His mouth is wide open, "I could ask you the same question, Elmo."

"Oh, really now?"

"Yes, this my home." What? What the—
"You're trespassing."

"Trespassing… yeah I am, so I'm gonna go…" I say and turn to look at the wall. I'm looking for some footing. Something to help push me up and over this wall fucking quickly. Never expected to see this guy again, let alone here.

"Is that how you got in here? Clever… you… were you trying to get a scoop? A story better than that lot out there—"

"—Hmm—"

"—My Dad's giving them nothing, so figures. Didn't realise you worked for the press—"

"—Wait, hang on. Did you just say Dad? As in your Dad is…"

"My Dad is the Prime Minister, yes."

Oh shit. I fucked Boris Johnson's son into oblivion in a Weatherspoons toilet.

Yikes…

Wait… Hang on a sec.

Didn't man's bring me to a Labour party gathering during our Tinder meeting? Didn't man's use me as a Labour party living mascot because I'm all red and furry? Didn't man's sit there and chat shit with me at the pub about his said Daddy-kins? Talk about batting for the other team, huh?

There's a little traitor in camp Johnson, aye? *Would you look at that.*

"Did you find what you were looking for?"

"Looking for?" I ask back. I'm still looking for my footing to get the fuck outta here, I don't know what he's on about.

"A scoop, no?" Oh. He thinks I'm a reporter. Yeah right, but it's better he continues to think that, honestly. He can't find out I just planted a bomb in his house.

That'd be bad.

Like he will find out eventually, when it goes off. But till then, it's gotta be hush, hush. So for now, meet Elmo, the reporter.

I turn around and look at him, "I don't know if I should be telling you that. You're the enemy. You're a Johnson."

"Don't you remember how we met?"

"Yeah. Tinder."

"And… " He begins, looking at me pointedly. "Where'd I take you?" Ah, right. He's talking about the Labour stuff.

"Ooooh, I see… and your point?"

"The point is, I'm not your enemy. If anything — you're mine."

"Yours?" I ask, baffled. "What do you mean, I'm yours?" Apollo is tapped, like I knew that before from the last time I saw him, but what he said just now. That's it, the icing on top of the cake. He's completely, positively tapped.

"Y-You at the spoons, y-y-ou…" I can't believe I didn't realise he was BoJo's son before. He's defo inherited that Johnson trait of mumbling and stumbling through the English language. I'm assuming man was Eton educated like his father, and his father before him. One of the most elite and expensive educations money can buy, yet they produce people who can't string actual sentences together. Like father, like son.

"I what?" Apollo takes a deep breath in. "I what, mate?"

"Y-You. You made me your b-bitch."

"Oooooh, so *that's* what this is about, huh? You brought that upon yourself," I say. He takes a step back, further into the garden. There's a bush behind him.

He opens his mouth like he wants to say something, but closes it again. Pussyo. "If you've got something to say just say it. Now's your chance," I tell him.

"How comes you haven't text me back? Not once."

"I was busy," I answer. It's not *exactly* a lie— I deleted his number. I didn't wanna see that wet-wipe again. For what reason? Release, sure, but there's plenty of other people for that. I don't know.

This guy was so pathetic. So beneath me, I couldn't help but treat him so… cruelly?

Damn, for me to be admitting to myself I was cruel to someone— the actual situation must've been *hella* bad. Oh well, what happened, happened init?

What I do remember very clearly was feeling control. Feeling like nothing could stop me.

Thinking about this is making me wanna smile though.

Shit.

I really don't have time for this right now, even if it's my own fucking crazy.

"Oh," he says looking down at his fiddling hands. He's a grown man but he looks like a fucking kid. Man needs to get a grip. "I-I wanted to ask you if we could…"

"Could what?"

"Could come to… an arrangement?" He asks. Arrangement? What's this guy on about. Do I even have time for this drawn out conversation— the swarm of ACTUAL reporters won't be keeping Boris occupied forever. Not to mention, he's gonna run out of tea and biscuits eventually. By then, I need to be the hell away from here.

Unless I want to be blown to smithereens. Which is a no.

"What do you want? Speed this up, I need to leave."

"I-I wanted to ask if… if… I could be your slave and you… if you'd be my master…" The guy is as red as me. Well who wouldn't be embarrassed after saying something like that?

Urm…

Is this guy serious? I guess anyone can be a masochist but bruh…

I never thought this would happen, but I guess anything's possible nowadays. I really shouldn't be surprised. Just as he's tapped, this bloody world is too. So… of course the wet-wipe I fuck in a Spoons toilet is gonna be having fantasies of him being my fucking slave.

"You wanna be… my slave?" He nods, and takes another step back. "You wanna be *my slave*?" I step towards him. He takes another one back, but this one was *too* back.

He stumbles backwards falling into the bush behind him.

I haven't had my blem yet… but I could give him a little taste, right? A little quick-y, I've got a little slave here and I wanna take him for a spin. What my mans don't know is that his house is about to be blown up.

He might never look the way he does now, today. He might not even exist past today. *Oh boy.* That boy makes me feel like so much more, because he's so small. He knows so little, if only he knew why I was really here today, right here, right now.

He probably thinks it's his lucky day, that Fate plopped his best fuck into his back garden. O fate, how twisted you are, everything is way too messed up. Everything in this world is so small. Everything's as connected as the fibre-optic thingy sending internet signals here, there and everywhere.

"Well, it's your lucky day," I smirk and pounce on him. He's like a dog on heat.

I'm crushing his body, under mine. I grab his mouth with one paw, and I bring my face close to his. He closes his eyes. I give him a long hard kiss.

He's melting under me. I'm pressing myself harder into him and the lower we fall into the bushes. They're thorny, who knows what the fuck kinda plants these are, but fuck. They sting. I can feel them scratching thin littles lines all over my limbs and back.

I remove my lips from his and muffle instead. I stick my fisted fingers inside, gagging him. Sometimes there's real benefits to being red and furry, am I right?

He's writhing underneath me, he looks like he wants to moan and cry at the same time. I take another quick survey of the garden and where we are in relation to the driveway where the reporters are. If he started screaming and moaning here… they *might* hear.

We need to go further down, so I can hear him turning into my little bitch once again. Spoons toilet is coming to mind. He was one loud motherfucker. If anyone had walked into the loo stall next to ours, they would've clammed up in pain. Tryna pee but getting a bloody stiffy instead. I pull out my fist from his mouth and grab the back of his collar on his shirt instead.

I step out of the bushes, my arm outstretched like a leash. I start walking along the line of bushes going into the depths of the garden— away from prying ears— with my pet in tow.

Just like any other dog owner walking their pet. It's just another day in the park. It's just another walk along the line.

As I'm dragging him through the bushes, my paw is getting cut over and over again, but I don't care. I'm probably bleeding. I look down at my flesh-steel grip on his collar and would you look at that. There are red smudges coming from my clasp.

We come to the end, the last bush of the line. Apollo looks like a bloody mess, all and white and red all over. His mouth gapping open, tongue hanging limply.

He's panting. *He's* out of breath?

I'm the one who just had to drag his sorry arse all the way here…

For fuck's sake. I let go of his collar, and he falls into the depths of bush.

I step over him, and he's looking up at me, panting. He looks so scared and…

I'm loving it.

I lower myself down into the bush—the thorns are already digging into my legs. Now they're poking into my butt. I grab Apollo's waistband and rip the cotton off him. He opens up his legs automatically the moment they're freed.

Yet they're tangled in the web of thorns. I see the blood dripping from his calves onto the leaves.

The slow drips staining the flowers.

SHOVE.

I thrust myself into him, he gasps for air.

PANT.

I penetrate faster, he's trying to grip everything and anything. He's clawing at the thorns, leaves and flowers around him. Crushing everything, everything, everything.

SHOVE.

"Haah," he moans.

I go HARDER, and he starts… *laughing?*

And as I go, he gets LOUDER and LOUDER and LOUDER.

He shouldn't have this much fucking breath. I take my right paw to his mouth and push down, HARD.

BANG.

"Mmmph!"

"Shut. Up." His head hits the dark soil, I continue to fuck him. Digging him. This is the best burial he can hope for, he's literally laying libations down early with all that blood for his very own memorial.

His moans continue at the same volume as before. The ground clamping gag did nothing. Slave has too much life. Too much energy. He's too lost in this. Too lost in me.

I inch my paw down lower on his face, and lightly rest it on his throat. His teary eyes lock on me.

THRUST.

Gasp.

PRESS.

My paw grips his neck harder.

Pant.

SHOVE.

PANT, PANT, PANT.

His tears streaming down his face have mixed with the soil. Dirt all over his face. What a dirty mess.

SHOVE.

Gasp.

THRUST.

GASP. His eyes roll back into his skull, like the best high of life. He's cumming, his dick spraying everywhere like a sprinkler, all the bush coated in him.

As I continue to fuck him it faces me, and it squirts all over me.

Great.

I penetrate him even FASTER, and choke him HARDER.

I'm getting so close to nutting, so I choke him some more and fuck him some more, that is…

Till I feel his neck go limp in my paw.

I look at his face, his eyes are still in the back of his skull. I pull out and stand up. He's just laying there, as limp as his dick.

Don't tell me…

Naaaa, he can't be…

Don't tell me he's… *dead?*

Shit then.

THIRTEEN

Fuck. Fuck. Fuck.

What the fuck just happened? How can someone just die during a beat like that? Man said he wanted to be my slave. If he couldn't handle it he should have never been like— I wanna be your slave.

I'm looking at the bush I left him in as I run. I can hardly even see him— he's basically hidden par the bloody legs sticking out from the sides.

Now, this is just gonna cause problems. I need to get out of here. I need to get the fuck out of here right now. *Shit.*

I'm stumbling out of the bushes, thorns are digging into my legs. They're bleeding but it doesn't matter. I need to get out of here. Nobody's gonna see the blood anyway, I'm red and blood's red anyways... but people can't see me. If people see me— I'll draw attention.

I don't even know if he's alive right now. I don't care. Fuck. I made a mistake. I made a stupid fucking mistake. I should've left after I planted the bomb. I deleted the wet-wipe for a fucking reason... because he's pathetic. I— I can't— SHIT.

Why? Why? Why? Why the fuck did I— Why did I have to just—

NO.

It was necessary…? I need to stop lying to myself. The thing is with pathetic people, sometimes you just can't help but take the piss— because most of the time they're already a piss-take… However, I might have just killed the Prime Minister's son. Well, at the very least I left him for dead, if he isn't already. But… he likes it rough…

He— He did at Weatherspoons… *right?*

He…

I'm…

No.

No… I'm not a mur—

NO.

There's no way. If anything I'm a sorta sadist then, that's gotta be it. I… I just don't know. I like pain.

I love pain.

It makes me feel alive. I don't always cum when I'm not feeling it like with the twins, you get me. I felt good though. I like dying. It makes me feel alive. Sure there's a thin line but…

Naaaaa no way. There's no way. There's no way that I… Did… I go too far?

Did I go too far? There were tears streaming from his eyes, and I'm pretty sure he was bleeding left, right and centre but he came nonetheless.

I've got his cum splattered all over me. Drying like sticky yogurt.

No. He liked it. There's no denying it. He enjoyed it. The screaming, the laughing, if I'm sick then he's sick too. What type of man doesn't defend himself if he doesn't want it? Doesn't like it?

It takes two to do the devil's tango. I can't dance alone. If I crossed the line of no return— I didn't do it alone. And it's not the first time we danced the devil's tango. I'm sure he was fully aware of what a second shag with me would be like, considering our first time in the pub toilets. Rough. He was aware. He shouldn't have followed me if he didn't want it, but he did so that means he missed my red stallion.

He probably couldn't find someone else after me that gave it to him as good as me. People that I fuck should count themselves lucky.

I finally get out of the garden, and turn my head around all sides. Apollo's legs are poking out of the bushes like twigs. All bent, scratched and worn-out. He looks pretty dead to me.

He's probably just… unconscious. He'll get up eventually or the gardener might just fetch him tomorrow or something… right? Yeah, of course. The gardener, fucking fancy posh Tory twats. He'll be just *fine.*

That wet wipe owes me his life. If his little Daddy found out he was secretly pushing for Labour… Political suicide for BoJo, but then again there's been so many fucking things he's done that should've been political suicide and YET *somehow* he's managed to survive. Nothing's gonna knock him off at this point. From tryna— naaa *ACTUALLY* sacrificing the country's population in favour of the economy during a global pandemic… Brexit, the miserable four year divorce of a shambles… Lowkey tryna sell off the NHS to Trump… Oh, let's not forget the little kid he's got from his affair like a decade ago with that architect… Not to mention so many other things… He actually thinks offering some tea and biscuits are gonna solve the world's problems, yeah right— *that bloody fucking twat.* Point is, maybe finding out Boris Johnson can't actually keep his camp conservative might actually do some sorta damage… at the very least Apollo won't be very liked in camp Johnson.

I'm laughing. Fuck. I'm laughing even more. I need to shut up. Can't draw attention… can't draw attention… but…

Fuck.

Apollo was laughing, crying and screaming like a bitch. Might actually be my favourite bitch so far. He's so weak, *I love it.* Shit I'm laughing so hard my stomach is starting to hurt, fuck. But he's fucking lucky he gotta a taste and yet… he *always* becomes a waste.

That waste of space is living in my head rent free right now. Naaaa fuck this I don't wanna think about him anymore.

Apollo is cancelled and sex is sex. That's it— Full-stop.

I give one last look down the entry of the garden from the corner of the backside of the house. Seems there's still cars and shit out front. Which means the driveway it still probably full of reporters? Can't go that way, the quicker way I mean.

Gotta find another way… Driveway… Wall… Driveway… Wall… and wall, it is then.

The way I came. Where I was before Mr. wet-wipe found me. Bloody hell, what a fucking day.

I do a quick take of where to put my foot and decide on some pile of neatly stacked bricks. Someone was planning some building work, aye? Well, right now thank you for building my escape, mate. Whoever you are.

I haul myself up and over the wall, then I jump down.

BAM.

I'm in the neighbour's garden again. I jog on out of here. I wanna have that blem, and *boy* do I need it. After all this fucking shit, I can't believe I managed to find the time to have a freaky quickie with Apollo but not have a blem. Bruv. Where are my priorities at? Not here, with me— *clearly.*

I walk out of the garden and onto the main road, the media circus is still there but their not gathered around in the middle of the lawn anymore. Seems like Boris has gone inside. Good thing I got out of there when I did then or he would've caught me red-handed, that wouldn't have been good now, would it?

I cross the road and sit down cross-legged under a tree that's on the pavement, open my satchel and start rolling.

Should I detonate it now? I've finished rolling now, so I take my first drag.

I take out my trap phone and open up the contact info for Homerton b.

Exhale.

He's gotta be inside right now... probably.

Inhale.

I press the call button.

There's hardly any reporters outside on the lawn anymore. The majority are getting into their cars and getting their shit into vans. Well it's about to not be a wasted journey for them...

BOOOOOOOOOOOOM.

Exhale.

BANG.

Heads whip in alarm to the house. The windows shattered, smoke is rising. Alarms are going off.

SCREAMS.

The media circus has commenced again, worse than it ever was before. Camera men are running out of their vans, stumbling and running to gather themselves. Loud twittering on phones, probably calling 999. Some reporters are screaming, some keeping their composure while trying to film the scene. Cameras are flashing, microphones are flying.

I dash my finished blem on the floor and head to the station. It's time to go. Time to go back home, to London.

My job is done.

About forty minutes later I'm on the train trying to block out people talking. I just wanna sleep, it's been a long day and all this madness isn't helping. There's some woman with her baby that just won't stop crying and her little toddler that won't stop running up and down the carriage, screaming.

What a headache. I would kill for a zoot right about now. Too bad you can't smoke on trains. For fuck's sake. I'm just tryna get home.

I wonder if Boris got caught in the explosion, I mean I hope he was. I don't wanna really think about if he wasn't, you get me. Oh well, if not I did it. I let the bomb go off. So that's something, right?

I guess all I'd have to do is look at the news on my actual phone but I kinda don't wanna know at the moment, because the moment I see the result… I might be walking dead meat…

Before I got into the station I snapped the trap phone's sim card in two and then dashed it the bin on the way in. I've seen enough TV shows to know I probably shouldn't keep that shit on me. Considering I just bombed the Prime Minister's yard— they're bound to have a deep and likely costly investigation into this.

Looking for good old me. Although I'm at the bottom of the pyramid scheme, I don't really know wagwan. I'm just tryna survive. I owe a lot of bad people. Well, not after today it seems. That debt is no longer and I feel so fucking free.

I love it. I'm fucking loving it. That dead weight's been lifted off my shoulders. I only hope Boris is fucking dead, then that'll actually be true.

The ringing of my proper phone takes me out of daydream, I take my eyes off the green English countryside I'm staring at mindlessly on train to see it's Oxi. What does she want?

"Hey Oxi," I say into the phone.

"E-Elmo…" she says, sniffling. Is the girl crying? Why's everyone crying these days? Jeeze. First Mazzy, then that wet-wipe and now her.

"Wagwan?"

"I'm still in Paris."

I didn't ask but, "O.K?"

"And Jezza— he—"

"—He's what?"

Silence.

"He tested positive for Corona," she whispers.

She's crying because he got COVID-19? All that talk about her not liking him back might have been complete bullshit if she's in tears over man getting a bloody cold.

"Well, it's not the end of the world, right? It's just a cold, he'll be alright—"

"—We're in some hospital right now, it's not looking good. He's on a ventilator." She cuts in.

Shit. That means… it's bad. Man can't breathe without a machine, huh?

Fuck if Jezza's actually that bad, lying in some hospital with Frenchies— maybe I should get tested. Yikes, do I even have time for that right now? How do I even *get* tested? Man this country is really behind on everything compared to other countries. Good thing leadership might actually be changing tonight. *Fingers crossed.*

"Are you positive too?" I ask.

"Nah, I'm not but you should get tested though. We all shared so much shit last week," she says. I know she's right. I can't even count everything we shared, drinks, zoots... fuck.

"What happened though? You lot were fine, when Mazzy and I left."

"A couple of days later, Jezza started getting a sore throat. We chalked it down to smoker's cough though, you get me. Then all of a sudden he was struggling to breathe, so I took him to A&E. Turns out he had Rona and here we are, init." She explains.

There's shuffling on the phone, I can hear beeping and machines going crazy.

What's going on?

"Oxi?"

No response, just strange mechanical sounds, till I hear a shrill. It's her.

"JEZZA!"

Wait, is she with him right now?

"Oxi, what's happening?"

LOUDER machine sounds.

Patter.

STOMP.

Patter.

STOMP.

There's people entering the room. Now I'm hearing French. Shit then…

Is Jezza—

"—Help him, please," Oxi cries.

—Jezza *is* dying.

Now I'm hearing the heart-rate monitor, sounds like a rollercoaster of a heart beat, that line decline's sounding as steep as the Eiffel Tower.

BEEP. BEEP. BEEEEEEEEEEEP.

BANG, CLINCK, BANG, CREAK.

Someone's doing CPR, I can hear someone counting up in French.

BEEP. BEEP. BEEEEEEP.

1, 2, 3…

"JEZZA!"

BEEEEEEEEEEEEEEEP…

Silence.

Screams. It's Oxi.

Jezza's dead.

Fuck. I need to get tested, seems like this COVID-19 shit *is* real.

FOURTEEN

Since Jezza's dead, and Mazzy and I were with him last week... not only do I need to get tested but so does Mazzy. I take out the trap phone to give him a call but there's no contact numbers.

Oh, shit. Were the details saved onto the sim card? Well that's in the bin in bloody Oxfordshire.

Stupid me, didn't think to memorise his number either. Great.

Guess I've got no choice. Gotta head to Mazzy's yard, what a trek.

Although I said I'd be heading to Mazzy's yard. The first thing I do when I'm back in London is walk into a Tesco's and get the cheapest Prosecco bottle they have. I think it'll be nice to celebrate the fact I've *finally* done my job.

Eventually I get to the outside of Mazzy's yard after about twenty minutes and press on the buzzer.

I wait for a bit, and there's nothing. Is he not in? Shit. I thought he would be... Does he even still live here? Fuck, it's probably been a few years since I've been here. I just assumed he still lived here. I should've asked him when I saw him in France— instead of asking irrelevant questions like, if he was seeing someone? Why did I even wanna know? Bruv, I'm not some yummy mummy gossiping over her son's rugby match.

I press the buzzer again and finally I hear some shuffling behind the door. Mazzy's coming.

The door opens, but it's not Mazzy.

"Doja?" What the fuck is she doing here?

"Elmo, long time no see," she says and opens the door wider for me to come in.

"Where's Mazzy at?" I ask her. She nods to the living room, and starts walking there. I follow suit and sure enough there's Mazzy on the sofa.

He looks kinda rough though, not gonna lie.

"Elmo?" He croaks. Oh boy, he don't sound good at all.

"Yeah… I didn't have your number so I came here. Needed to talk to you. I brought a bottle," I say wagging it my paw.

He gives me a light smile, "Sit down mate." He pats the cushion next to him on the sofa. Doja's disappeared.

"Don't mind if I do," I reply sitting down.

"So… Elmo, wagwan? It's rare for you to want to talk. Especially after what went down in France."

"Remember Jezza?" I start. Mazzy looks at me, puzzled. Jeeze, was man was that invisible or was Mazzy just that fucked? "You know man, Oxi's mate. The English guy…"

"Oh, yeah. What about him?"

"He's dead." Mazzy just looks at me blankly.

"That's sad and all, but what's that got to do with me? You didn't just come all the way over here to my yard to tell me some guy I don't really know or give a shit about is dead."

"Well, actually I did—"

"—You did? Why?"

"Because he had Corona, and now he's dead. We were all chilling together in Paris last week or have you forgotten already?"

"Oh. No wonder I feel like death then. I've probably got Rona. Doja's been taking care of me and my cold this last week. I literally feel like I can barely move," he says and then proceeds to cough.

Shit maybe he does have Corona… Fuck, if he does and the fact Jezza's already dead…

I might actually have Covid. *Shit*. Although I haven't felt sick, not one bit so far… Maybe I'm the lucky one?

"Wait, hang on. Doja's been taking care of you?" I ask, he just nods. "How comes you two even know each other?"

"We met on Tinder a while back. She's nice."

I find myself nodding in response, it's not like I wanna shatter man's fragile image of her when he could be on his deathbed like Jezza. Probably not the best time to mention I'm pretty sure her brother's in love with her — in an incest-type way.

Speak of the devil, Doja comes back into the room holding some mugs. "Coffee?" She offers me and Mazzy.

"Na, I'm good. I've got some Prosecco," I decline. It's time to open the bloody bottle actually. Can't believe I've been sat here chatting without a drink. After this fucking day. I wonder how I'm not asleep. Shit, that reminds me.

"Turn on the TV," I say. Mazzy grabs the remote and some random E4 show is playing. "Put on BBC News."

Video footage is playing, it's Boris' wrecked house. Damn, I really did a number on the Johnson's and

I can't help but grin. The screen has a banner at the bottom, "BREAKING NEWS: Terrorist attack at PM's residence."

Mazzy turns to look at me, "No wonder you're grinning like some creep."

"Well you are the one that told me, today was the day mate. You good?"

He's silent for a moment. Then I see some spark of recognition in him, "Oh shit, yeah. I forgot I even did that."

"Mazzy, are you sure you've just got a cold? Something don't seem… *right?* You don't just forget things like that man. Last time you saw me, I thought you never wanted to talk to me again and now your acting like nothing's up?"

"What's the big deal man? You're giving me a headache," he grumbles. I pull my head back to get a better look at him. I'm squinting and I just clocked. Man's not sick, man's high.

For fuck's sake.

For him to be this high, Jesus. It's like me, sure. It's not like Mazzy though. Yeah sure, he has fun— but he was always the type to do shit at a motive or something specific— you get me? He was always a social drug taker, but for him to be like this… he had to have started the sesh, solo after Paris then just continued.

I can handle that shit, I can function. *Oh Mazzy, Mazzy, Mazzy…*

He can't even get up, has to call over some girl from Tinder to look after him. Well, I guess I can't judge him or… *them*. Seems like they've known each other a while.

"When they gonna tell us if he's dead?" Mazzy asks.

159

"Mate, I got no idea. Probably in a few hours—maybe days? Who knows…"

Mazzy bringing up wagwan with BoJo has turned something into stomach bile, I don't feel too good. I need a fucking blem, now. Instead I open the bottle and chug some of it down.

"Woah easy there, why don't you slow down, Elmo?" Doja says. I give her a, 'are you serious' look.

You know what, fuck it. Me giving a shit about Mazzy's image of Doja? She's crazy and he's gotta open his fucking eyes. Man's not dying, man's high—*remember.*

"So when did you two meet? Never would've thought I'd find you lot together." I begin. Doja decides to sit down cross-legged on the floor in front of us for this. Must be a long story. She motions for me to pass her the bottle, so I do.

She takes a swig of her coffee, then a swig of the Prosecco. Ew, I hope the coffee's cold or else… Naaa—just no.

"So… someone gonna answer my question?"

"I met Mazzy a couple times before COVID-19 started," she says. Ahh, now that makes sense, that was when I ghosted her because she'd become way too clingy. Girl was defo in love with me, and I just couldn't deal with the extra hassle that came with. Don't even think I can deal with that now, to be honest. I haven't changed much.

Mazzy beside me, is looking at Doja with a soft smile. One *I've* never seen before. *He likes her.* Well, obviously or else she wouldn't be answering his fucking front door. That's not it. *There's something else to this.*

Can't put my finger on it. Lemme poke the bear, and see what else I can find out. I need a bigger picture. "How's your brother?"

Doja takes another swig from the bottle before replying, "I haven't been back home in about two, three weeks that's what."

Oh, I wonder why…

Pfftt, yeah right. I know exactly why. It doesn't take a genius to figure that whole family needs to see a therapist, like ASAP.

"Dojo's got problems, b. Although, you're not so innocent yourself but he's on another level though."

"You're right about that. Do you know how awkward things were after that threesome? Terrible. *Absolutely terrible.*"

"Well, what do they always say about threesomes? It's best with strangers or only two people that kinda, vaguely know each other with someone that's a stranger to either one or both. You lot are fucking siblings. Even my fucked up head, thinks your dynamic must be… *strained.*" I say.

"Bruv," Mazzy starts. The conversation's getting a bit much for her. She finishes the bottle. I take that as my cue to start rolling a blem. "You lot had a threesome together with her brother? That's fucked up." I take a drag of my blem. Doja doesn't say anything. "That's why you came to stay with me at first then, isn't it?"

Exhale.

Doja looks down at the floor. She's embarrassed and ashamed. "Don't be like that, it's alright— I don't care—"

"—You don't care that I slept with my brother?"

Inhale.

"—I don't care that you've done some fucked up shit. It's not that deep— we've all done fucked up shit…" he drools on and looks at me. Yeah, of course he's looking at me— I'm VERY aware of the fucked up shit he's done and involved in. Clearly, man got me involved with terrorists. "The point is... the point is I like you, the you that's lived a little. The you's that's done this and that. Look, if that fucked up shit hadn't have happened, you never would have needed a place to crash. You probably wouldn't have hit me up. Everything happens for a reason, b."

Exhale.

Who's the person talking next to me? What's this lovey-dovey vibe I'm getting here...? What exactly is going on with them? Is this really Mazzy, since when the fuck did he sound like *this?* Maybe he's high or maybe he's high-key in love with her but...

Why don't I like it? I shouldn't care. I really shouldn't...

"Maz..." Doja whispers. She's trembling on the floor. I can see her hand going white because she's gripping the empty Prosecco so hard. "I-I'm so glad that... I'm so glad you've been what you've... *been* these last few weeks. I don't think I've ever felt like this before, Maz."

I turn to Mazzy, "Is this who you were seeing? Why you were evading my questions before, in France?"

"To be honest, Elmo. I don't know what we are —"

"—We're just doing what we're doing and that's that," Doja interjects. Look at them, finishing each other's sentences. They're so cliché, it's making me sick.

"It's chill," Mazzy adds.

The fuck is this? Guess it's really my business. No, actually it isn't at all. I'm just bothered. For what reason I don't know. Maybe it's because I know Doja used to like me, and it seems like she's moved on— but I don't really want her. It's Mazzy, she's doing whatever that is with him. Mazzy and I have a fucked whatever we are too. Just last week in that French field fuckery— he kinda seemed almost like... I don't wanna even think about this again.

Shit.

But did Mazzy have feelings for me? I know he learned a lesson when he tried to school me, I think I crushed whatever the fuck it was, he clearly felt about me.

Yet… I don't want to admit this, but I might have been wrong. Mazzy wanted me to care, to give a shit and some regard to him— *perhaps?* But I didn't, I pushed his buttons like I always do, I can't help it when it comes to him. It's just how it is now, and I don't know why.

But seeing him like this, with Doja is making me realise, that I done fucked up.

I *do* care.

I care… about Mazzy… I was wrong to push his buttons so far as to kill whatever it was he had for me. Worst of it all, I feel like I have FOMO right now— like when you miss a motive that sounded amazing.

I feel like I've missed out on him, and yet I don't even know what that could've been— or could've looked like… and I guess I'll never know, now. Maybe it would've been like with him and Doja that I'm seeing right now, before my very eyes… but that's bullshit— because Doja and I are very fucking different. She's all warm, with pasta, sunshines, rainbows with a dash of freak. I'm a crackhead, to put it in simple terms.

Is this jealousy or just me wanting what I can't have anymore? They were both my toys, that I played with, but now they're playing with each other without me.

What is this?

FIFTEEN

It's been a couple of hours since we finished watching Christian Bale's Batman trilogy. I can't believe I've spent the whole day here... but it's been actually— nice?

Maybe it's because Mazzy's here but we've been smoking up and chilling. It's been a while since I chilled with him and frankly, I missed this. THIS is what us in France should've been like, not whatever nonsense that was.

It's not everyday, I need to drive people mad....

Sometimes though... I just can't help it.

It's me we're talking about here. This crazy red, furry creature of a man. Am I even a man? Who knows, but I've got balls and a dick if that counts for anything anymore. Although it seems kind of irrelevant.

As per usual, with Doja's obsession with making fucking pasta... She cooked us some pasta, this time though she wasn't some table nazi like last time— with her and Dojo— but she was chill. Doja's *waaaaaay* more chill now. I guess it's true what they say, being in some sort of relationship can really change a person. She's not that annoying anymore, I don't know if that's down to Mazzy's influence or whatever else— but she's alright now.

Mazzy feel asleep after he had some of the pasta on the sofa while watching Batman and hasn't woken up since. Doja and I have been chatting shit about TV shows. She's recommending I invest in a Netflix subscription, but I just don't know.

I don't know how comfortable I am with knowing there's always gotta be p's in my account because Netflix is coming every month like a fucking period. Do I even have enough time to actually watch enough to make it worth it? I'd like to think I do but like… I can barely remember to fucking shower, you get me.

Anyways, I don't know how I got here but the sun's already come up. I realise I fell asleep on the floor, Doja's next to me. I look up and see Mazzy still dead asleep on the sofa.

Wow, man is *still* out like a light.

Doja gets up and goes to the kitchen. I take the rolling stuff next to me and start rolling a blem. What a good morning, aye? It's been a long while since I woke up like this. The sun is spilling into the living room from the massive windows. I can feel it warming my back. Damn must be a hot day.

I take my first drag and Doja comes back with three coffee cups. She places one down on the table (I'm assuming for when Mazzy wakes up), walks over to me and hands me one.

"Thanks," I say and take a sip. Fuck it's hot, but it's just right. Black, no sugar. Perfect for the morning with my blem.

Doja's just standing there blowing her coffee, clearly it's too hot for her, at the moment. She's got a dopey little smile on her face though, I follow her eyes and she's looking at Mazzy fast asleep on the sofa. How cute.

Inhale.

Doja walks over to the sofa and kisses Mazzy's forehead.

Exhale.

Her free hand goes to stroke his hair out of his eyes. "I made some coffee baby," she says.

No response. Damn man's in some deep sleep.

Inhale.

"Mazzy? Wake up!" She says, and I chuckle. Yeah good luck with that Doja, Mazzy's known to be a deep sleeper. He once slept for like two days after this next up rave we went to a couple years back.

Exhale.

I take a swig of coffee, and Doja's shaking him now. Well, now that's gonna wake him up and he's not going to be happy… even with the coffee waiting for him.

Inhale.

"Mazzy?" She calls. She brings her head closer to his, is she gonna kiss him awake?

Exhale.

To my surprise, she doesn't. Her head doesn't get closer, her lips don't touch his. What's she doing? Her hand slowly goes to his face instead. Then, softly and slowly to his neck.

CRY.

"Elmo…"

"What?"

CRIES.

"M-Mazzy—"

"—What? He's sleeping, I know I can see that b—"

"—No," she whispers. I barely heard *that.*

"No? What do you mean no?" I ask. Girl's gone mad.

"He's— He's not sleeping—He's—" I really don't get what she's on about. It's such a nice morning for her to wanna ruin it with nonsense. I don't know what time it is, but the sun's up, we just woke up and I'm having my morning blem with coffee. It's too early for this, I know *that*.

I take another drag of my blem, Doja's started crying and whimpering. Jeeze. What *is* going on?

"Doja, come on. I dunno wagwan but it's too early for the waterworks b. At least wait till midday like — if Maz's not awake now, you ain't gonna make him wake up because you're crying. Man's tired, let him sleep."

Inhale.

"L-Let him sleep… *f-f-forever?*" She cries.

Exhale.

"*Forever?* What the *bloody hell* are you on about now? No, seriously what the fuck is going on with you? Did you just start your period or something?"

Inhale.

"No I—"

"What is it then?" She's starting to piss me off now.

Silence.

Oh so now she's got nothing to say? She's just looking at Mazzy mindlessly. She looks hella fucking sad. Didn't realise her mood wasn't the only thing that changed. What happened to the dopey smile she had when she was staring at him five minutes ago?

Exhale.

Bruv, emotional females are scary.

"Mazzy's dead." The blem in my mouth drops. What?

I stand up and go over there, coffee in tow. There's Mazzy lying on the sofa. I put my paw under his nose, and she's right— there's no air on my fur. He isn't breathing.

"Shouldn't we do CPR or something?" I ask her. She shakes her head. "You sure?"

"I think it's too late. Who knows when he died? He's been sleeping so long…" *Shit*. She's right about that. Don't tell me man's died during Batman. That was last night, but somewhere around the second film is when I remember him… being awake…

Being alive.

CRY.

Mazzy's… dead.

CRIES.

He's… *Fuck.*

What.

The.

Fuck.

What the *actual* fuck?

"What do you even do when someone just… *dies?*" I ask.

Doja sniffles, and I've got nothing to do except take a swig of my coffee since I dropped my blem earlier. I realise as I'm holding the cup that I'm shaking.

Shit, shit shit.

Fuck this. Why am I pissing myself off?

Mazzy's—

I'm allowed. I'm—

Fuck.

I—

Mazzy...

There's no more Mazzy. I'll never see him again. I'll never get to—

Shit. I done fucked up. I don't even wanna think about *all this* right now— before all the regret piles on me in tonnes. Shit.

"Let's call 999. I can't think of anything else we're meant to do when—*this*— happens." Doja replies, finally. She picks up her phone and calls.

She's sipping her coffee while she's on the phone to the emergency services; she's giving them Mazzy's address and whatnot— and I'm rolling another blem.

I need a fucking blem. Right. Now.

I sit down and I'm still trying to roll, but it's not working. Why can't I roll? Shock? Probably. How do you just die like that? I didn't even get to…

Fuck I wish I had straights right about now.

I feel a hand on my shoulder, and then another on the other. I look up, it's Doja. She's just looking down at me. She's wetting my face with her tears. I can feel her pressing her weight into me, through her hands.

I've become her walking stick, yeah? Girl's lost all her power, all her strength. I don't think she can even hold herself up right now. "Sit down," I tell her. She nods and uses me as her pivot to walk around to come in front of me.

She lets go and she starts falling. I thrust my paws out. My rolling stuff's fallen off my lap and onto the floor. I catch her hands mid-air and then proceed to use them as puppet strings and drape her over my legs and the floor gently.

Cry.

If she'd fallen, the way she was going she probably would've knocked her teeth out.

CRY.

Doja wraps her arms around my legs, and rests her head against my red fur. She's gripping them so hard, it's like she tryna cling onto the edge of a cliff.

CRIES.

My legs are becoming so damp, but I don't care.

It's O.K.

Well, no it isn't actually this whole thing is fucked and I don't understand what the fuck is going on but alas, for some strange and twisted reason— I don't feel like being a dick right now.

Even Doja, crying right now. She's making me wanna cry. I'm not sure why, but somehow it took Mazzy having to die for me to care about someone other than numero uno.

How fucked is that, huh?

SIXTEEN

Doja was crying on me for a good two hours. It was a struggle to open the door for the ambulance people when they came for Mazzy's corpse. They were knocking and knocking, calling out for someone to come, and I was trying don't get me wrong.

She was just clinging to my legs so hard, they couldn't really move. I never realised this girl weighed a tonne, or maybe it's my legs that are just hella weak. Not gonna lie, it's probably the latter.

By the time I'd gotten to the door to open it, they'd already busted it open. How I managed to get to fucking hallway with Doja clinging to my legs like some Toddler with separation anxiety is beyond me. I had to resist some mad urges to not kick her fucking face in and get her the fuck off of me— but it just didn't make sense you know. I put in effort, *real effort* at the start of her crying escapade you know, would've gone to waste if I'd just caved and stomped all over her like a slab of wood to go open the door, init.

Like that's not even the worse part the girl's been trying to fuck me for the last twenty minutes… I don't know what the fuck has gotten into her, but I'm NOT in any mood to be fucking.

Mazzy's dead.

She literally started slithering herself up me, and was kissing me. At first, I didn't even clock she was lipsing me till I woke up from my daze. At this point, I just kinda threw her off me and told her I had to go to Sainsbury's.

So…

Now I'm in Sainsbury's. Like, I get it— Mazzy, whatever he was to her is dead. I mean I even find this whole thing tapped— but like come on, tryna fuck me?

Considering last time I went anywhere near her, I was basically telling myself she's a fucking freak and was just like nah. Then I find her shacked up with Mazzy, and all up in each other's grill. I'm not one for morals and that— like, with my track record, *clearly*.

But bruv, that just don't feel right. What? Sue me. I don't feel like having sex right now. Not gonna lie, it's kinda fucked still that she—

Let's just chalk that up to her not thinking straight, right? We all go a… little crazy *sometimes*, and I know she's defo capable of being tapped. Maybe I should call her crazy twin brother to look after her— after this? Because I've got shit to do, well… not really, but I— I don't think I can deal with her crazy on top of the fact I'm probably gonna crazy too.

More so, than I clearly already *am* too, it seems…

Yeah. Can't be doing this nursing shit. Gotta nurse myself, methinks.

Of course I'm in the alcohol aisle. Might as well get some medicine, init? A bottle here, another there— Ooooouh there's flavoured gin. Let's grab that. I look down at my little basket, it's fucking heavy now. Well, of course it's filled to the brim with… *medicine.*

I'm about to turn the corner and grab some mixers when my phone starts buzzing. It better not be Doja calling— I swear down— I just need some peace like, bruv.

Thank fuck, it's Oxi. Although it's a FaceTime call. She never FaceTimes, guess there's a first-time for everyone, huh?

"Oxi? What's up?" I ask, she just looks down at me on the screen then moves back till I can't see her. I think she's put me on a chair or something. I can't really see anything yet, the screen is focusing…. focusing….

Oh shit.

I'm seeing a framed picture of Jezza, some flowers and a casket— with what I'm assuming is… Jezza. Damn, it's just death all around, ain't it?

Fuck me, do I even have the energy for this?

I take myself to the corner of the aisle and sit down, the beer crates are behind me. I grab a bottle of red from my basket and crack it open. Now's as good a time any. I've been waaaaaay too sober for this fucking shit. Mazzy's death, completely made me forget that Jezza died first, and from COVID-19 no less.

Shit I might be next… Bruv, I can't even think about that shit right now.

I take a long swig from the Bordeaux.

I look back the screen and deep there's like no one there. I can only see two people's backs and I'm assuming Oxi's somewhere there— like it's her fucking phone FaceTiming me, init. Logic.

Is she still in France? Honestly I don't even fucking know… churches all look the same from the inside. I've got no fucking clue.

I chug down some more wine, while I'm watching some woman come up to the casket. She falls on top of it and cries. Yup, I chug down some more.

"Excuse me, sir." Someone says. I look up, and it's someone that works at Sainsbury's.

"Umm hmm," I mutter. Looks like Oxi's crying over at the casket now. The priest looks kinda strange though, I can't tell if he's grimacing or smirking…

"You can't just drink here, sir. I know, believe me I know the queues are about 2 hours long right now — but you can't just give up—"

"—Give up? What are you on about?"

"If you don't get up, I'm going to have to call security to remove you— "

"—Remove me? But I'm trying to watch A FUNERAL here!" I shout and take another swig of wine.

"A funeral?" He asks, and I motion to my phone. The Sainsbury's person sits down next to me and grabs a beer from behind us and starts downing it.

About thirty minutes later, Oxi ends the call and the Sainsbury's person is balling next to me. They've drank quite a bit to be fair, but still. Man's came here to get away from Doja's antics. This lunatic is all snotty and mopey. He's bare tryna hug me.

Which is my cue to go.

I stand up and realise that where the Sainsbury's guy is sat there's about 2 packs of empty Stella's and a couple of empty wine bottles.

At least I don't have to be sober to deal with Doja anymore. I hope she's calmed down by now.

Well… here's to hoping.

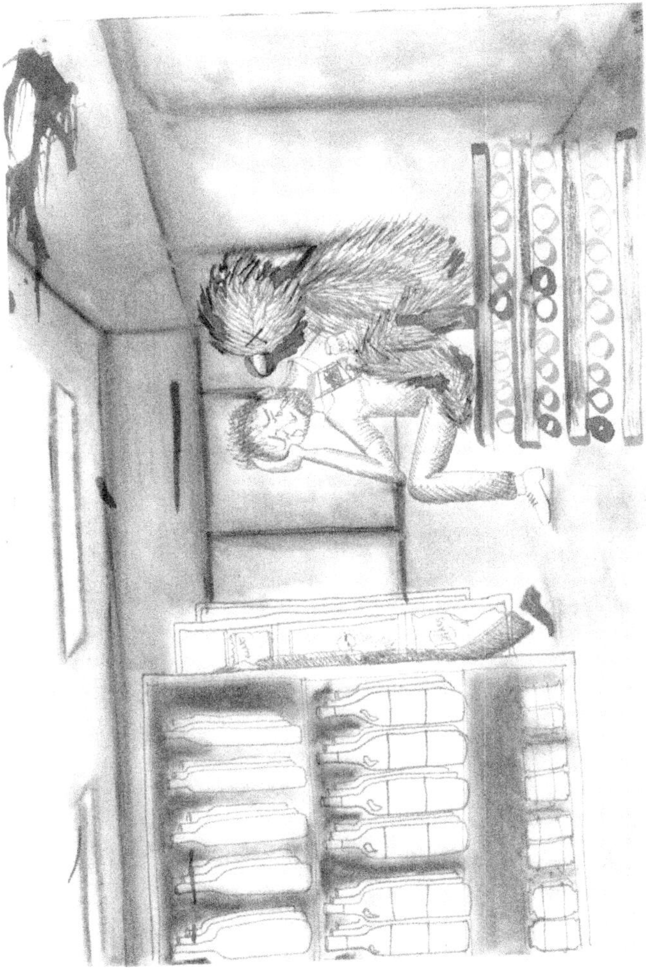

SEVENTEEN

I've been here two days now. I haven't left Mazzy's place since I got back from Sainsbury's and nor has Doja. We're currently sat on sofa where Mazzy died. I'm switching the channels and stop at BBC News, channel 1.

Oooouh. Looks like there's an update on Boris. I hope he's dead, or else I'll probably be as dead as Mazzy by the end of the week.

BREAKING NEWS, the headline reads on the screen.

"The explosion that occurred at the Prime Minister's residence has been concluded to be a terrorist attack. Unfortunately, the Prime Minister's son who was at the premises died on the way to the hospital. Our deepest condolences are with the Johnson family during this difficult time. The investigation is still ongoing, no organisation has yet to claim responsibility. Boris Johnson remains in critical condition, and has also tested positive for Coronavirus—"

"—Great, just fucking great, isn't it. He might actually die. Hopefully COVID-19 finishes him off." I say.

Corona *needs* to finish him off, for my sake. Or else...

"Yeah, Miss Rona is no joke. Bare people be dying." Doja adds. "Too bad about that friend of yours, that died in France."

"Yeah," I say. Oxi looked pretty devastated on FaceTime. "Did you get ahold of Mazzy's family yet?" I ask.

She sighs, "I tried the number for his mum that was on his phone—I called and it said the number didn't exist anymore, that I dialled the wrong number."

That's pretty fucked then. What's gonna happen when his family wonder where he's at?

He's bloody dead, for fuck's sake.

"Well, we're picking up his ashes today. You should leave a text or something. Does her contact info have her email there?" I ask.

"Yeah, I think so… I'm not sure lemme check." She bends over and grabs his phone. "It's here."

"O.K. pass it here," I say. She hands it to me, and I start typing.

To whom it may concern,

If you're looking for Mazzy, he got Corona and died. Nothing dodgy. Tried to call you but alas here I am writing an email. We're doing a scattering ceremony for him today— I know it's sad you won't be here and all… So we'll save you a couple grams of him. I'll probably be a goner soon too, but Doja's the one to bet that will stay alive— she looks after herself (well, kinda— somewhat, more than me anyways). So try find her to pick up your Mazzy grams, like you made him— you should get some of him, you get me. I'll write her contact details underneath. Well, yeah your son's dead, but he had a good time. We'll send another email later with a video or something for you to see where he's gonna be at, and resting— you know… in peace.

I pass the phone back to Doja, "Write your number at the end and send it." She does and I hear the sent sound.

Done.

A couple of hours later, Doja and I are at Hampstead Heath. This was the place Mazzy loved most. We had some good times here back in the old days. Just lounging around on those sunny summer days at the top of the hill overlooking the running tracks. All them times we used to chill here and look up at the sky and just bun. A couple beers, a couple girls. Younger times are always simpler times, aren't they?

We stopped by the Tesco before getting into the park and got some of Mazzy's favourite drinks. I also emptied out all of Mazzy's drug box under his bed into a little backpack I found in his room. It's not like he's gonna miss it now, anyways.

We plonked ourselves at the top, close to where everyone goes to pee but still on the grassy bit overlooking everything. By some strange miracle its really sunny right now. Doja's rolling a zoot and I'm smoking a blem while drinking a Stella.

"You know, if it wasn't for you— we— I mean Mazzy and I never would've got to where we did," she says sparking the zoot.

"What do you mean?" I ask, taking the last swig of Stella then taking another. "I thought you lot met on Tinder or something."

"Yeah, we did meet on Tinder. But like…"

I give her a 'go on' look, "…Like?"

"This is kinda cringe to say, and Mazzy never would've said, you get me. But like, he's gone now… We both met tryna get over someone else we were into."

"Ah, the classic— get under someone new to get over someone else. Oldest trick in the book," I add.

"Yeah, but here's the thing, Elmo. The person we were both tryna get over and basically forget… was you."

"Me?"

"Yeah, you."

"I knew you liked me, maybe a little too much — but I always made it clear. That I wasn't—"

"—I know, believe me I know, Elmo. I was young, dumb and stupid. I thought I had a lid on it but I didn't—"

"—clearly." I finish. "Wait. Are you trying to say Mazzy was trying to get over me? Back then… when you lot met?" I ask. She nods in response.

I did have my suspicions about Mazzy since the France trek because of everything that happened over there… but he… before…?

Fuck.

How could I have been so blind?

"So… you both got over me then, in the end? With each other?"

"Well, I know I did. I can't fully say the same about Mazzy. I know when I re-connected with him recently after whatever happened between you two in France— he was more… *committed?* Maybe that's not the right word… determined perhaps… *to let you go*. That's why it was so good with us at the end. I think I was probably falling in love with him, if I wasn't already…"

Yikes.

"I don't exactly know how to feel about that…" I begin and chug half the Stella down.

"Yeah, to be honest— I wouldn't either."

"Then why tell me, clearly Mazzy didn't want me to know all this—"

"—Yeah but, you're not stupid. One day you would've wondered, one day you'd have re-collected all your memories with him and thought shit, did Mazzy…"

She trails off. Little does she know I already did have—suspicions… but I haven't wondered.

I don't want to be in the sun the day I do. It should be a dark day. Not a day like today.

"…I've got a big mouth…" I hear her say at one point, but I've lost her. I ate a bunch of Mazzy's shrooms earlier when we got out of Tesco. Guess the blazing sun and alcohol are also playing their part.

I feel good though. I think Mazzy would've been happy that I feel good. I—

I wish Mazzy had just come out with it back then, about what Doja was saying a couple minutes ago… Although, if I'm being honest with myself I probably would've hurt him.

Let's be real.

I'm no fucking saint, nor was Mazzy for that matter neither. Or else man wouldn't have gotten me involved with bloody fucking terrorists, you get me. Bruv, to this day I don't even know the extent of his… *involvement* in stuff or like what he's *really* done. Maybe there was a time when I would've known but that time long came and passed as expressed by us both in France.

Doja's hand comes into my view. She waving a zoot all up in my face. I grab it off her and light it.

I look around at the Tesco bag of drinks we brought and it's nearly empty. There's just Mazzy's two whiskeys left. I look up at Doja, and she meets my eyes.

It's time. It's time to do this.

Fuck.

She opens her bag takes out Mazzy. He's still fresh from the cremation. I can't believe this is actually happening. That this is why we're here. I nearly forgot. She places Mazzy down, and takes a whiskey bottle. I take the other.

"Oh shit, I nearly forgot…" She says and rummages in her bag. She takes out her phone, rests it up against the bag and starts recording a video.

Oh, the email. Even I forgot bruv. What can I say though, you get scatter-brained when you're high. It be like that sometimes.

"This is for you mate," I say. I unscrew the cap and take a swig of whiskey. Then I stand up slowly, Doja follows suit. I pour the contents into the grass and then spray it up, down— everywhere. Like I'm peeing with a bent dick.

"I HOPE YOU LOVE IT MAZZY!" I shout at the top of my lungs. Some heads turn to us, but I don't care. This is Mazzy's time.

"I love you, Maz," Doja says looking out at the sun— almost like she's speaking to him. The way her eyes look lighter in the sun, and her skin warms under the sun. It's like Mazzy's saying it back. "I LOVE YOU!" She unscrews the cap and takes a shot in the cap. Then like me— she sprays it everywhere.

A golden libation, under the Mr. Blue Sky's golden waves.

We both reach down for Mazzy, holding him together. She opens him up, and we just stand there. We watch the wind take him slowly into the sun.

We're just seeing him float away, thousands of little specs glittering like Christmas lights on Oxford Street.

Mazzy…

Before he runs out I close his lid, so Doja can give him to his mum one day.

I look at the last of him in the sky, and I can feel my eyes watering away, escaping me— like Mazzy right now.

Goodbye, Mazzy.

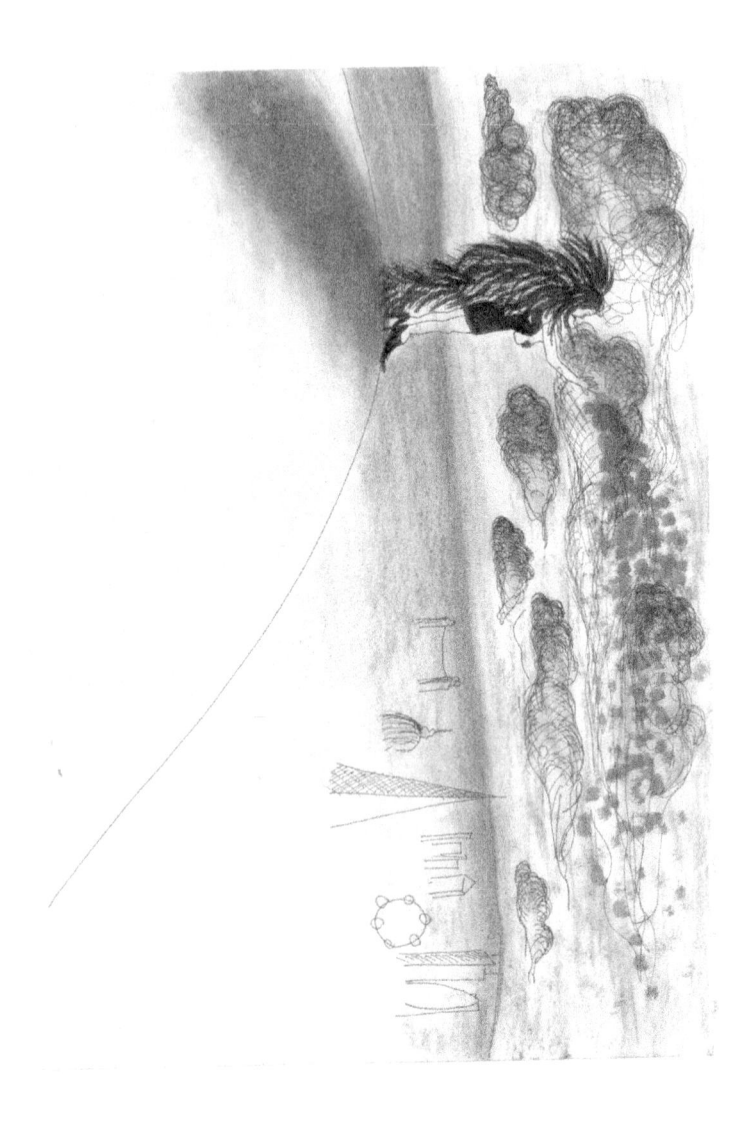

EIGHTEEN

I'm back in my shitty flat. High as shit, drunk as shit. I'm just gonna finish off everything I took from Mazzy's place. I still have the little backpack I packed with all his shit. I might as well put it all to good use, you know. He'd want that.

I can't fucking do this. I don't wanna think about anything at all.

Turns out Boris survived.

He fucking survived. That bloody rat. He just doesn't die does he? Whether it's a scandal or a bomb. For fuck's sake.

That's my death sentence right there. Mazzy's gone, he was my go-between and he's gone— *dead*. Caput. Nada. Dust.

What's more, now London's officially in a full-on lockdown. So being at home isn't that deep. The world's stopped. The streets are as empty and deserted as Paris was. At least there isn't a curfew like Paris though. That shit's peak.

Although, there's literally nothing going on. Nothing whatsoever. I don't know how the world can be this fucking cruel. Mazzy got COVID and died. Boris got it and he's A okay? Fuck that. Fuck this shit, man. Even Jezza died— he had his dead moments, sure. But... I would rather he be here than fucking Boris.

Mazzy and Jezza they were both young. Like not, young-young, but early twenties you get me? Boris? He's like five hundred, bruv.

This world fucking stinks.

I take a drag of my zoot and sway to the music playing. I'm listening to one of Mazzy's playlists from his Spotify profile. Isn't it weird how when people die, it's like they're still here because they still exist on socials?

Back in the old days, you die, you die. That's that. Maybe there'd be a painting or a picture or something. Socials are scary bruv, but right now I'm glad… because me choosing music right now— nope, NO.

My head hurts. It's whirling around, I'm not even sure it's working.

Did I forget to mention he had a couple pills in there, and I just downed them just now. A pink one, a blue one and yellow one. I've got no idea what they are — it's not like they come with labels, but if I was to take a guess MD and 2CB?

Everything's just spinning, but maybe I'm the one turning. I remember when I was last high in here— with Oxi and Jezza.

I wonder how Oxi is, seems like she was really torn at the funeral from what I saw. It seemed like she was close to his family too, well they were long-time friends before I met them… so it's not weird.

I feel kind of bad now, Jezza's dead and maybe Oxi *was* in denial. But seeing how she was crying for him and how horrible she looked, how her voice was cracking when we were on the phone call when he flatlined… maybe she did like him as more than a friend? Maybe Jezza did have a chance with her, but I didn't know it, nor did she.

But, Jezza… He'll never know now. That's what happens when you die, everything stops. You just run out of time. That's the sad truth of life, everything stops. Just like when your high stops, you get that nasty comedown.

I've been sober so little, I don't really remember what—how to function without… something. Fuck, this.

Just fuck it all.

There's times I've died. Or I think I've come close. During sex, it's the closest I come. It's the closest I come to anything at all these days.

Did it not take Mazzy having to basically fuck the shit out of me to make me realise that I do care— *did* care about stuff… about him?

But it's too late now. Is this what Oxi feels like right now, about Jezza? Full of regret and missed… whatevers? Is this what dread feels like?

Damn. I'm so stupid.

So.

Fucking.

Stupid.

I am wondering though, how that wet-wipe died? Was he already kissing death when I left him in the bush in the garden… or did he manage to get into the house and get caught up in the explosion? I guess I'll never know. It's a mystery.

Mysteries, they're such petty things. They draw you in, grab your attention then fly away like a magpie stealing your silver before you've had a chance to put them away. You just catch a glimpse but you're left needing more. More of the story. More of the person. The world of what if's are vast and long.

The never ending questions, that will replay forever and forever. Like every dawn that touches the day.

Mazzy will always be that misery, that mystery unsolved. Cold.

Fuck it, FUCK IT ALL.

What's the use? What's *my* use?

If only the me from when I first met Oxi and Jezza could see me now… I wouldn't believe it. I can't even be bothered anymore. I don't wanna fuck, I don't wanna cum.

I—

I— I'm losing my fucking shit.

What is this? What is this *madness*? It's drowning me, my head's heavy. Yet I'm light, and empty like the nonsense influencers selling fake lives on social media. A big parody. A big fucking farce.

Ironic, isn't it?

I've had my cake, with all those crazy beats, highs and peaks. Something is aching inside me, not the type of something I can feel piercing in me if it was a knife. It's almost like it's not there, like… *I'm crazy*. This numbness is crippling.

I'm empty and void.

All my highs used to make me want to party and fuck. Living was easy… but now I'm just an aching soul.

Damn.

NINETEEN

I'm lost. If I was feeling numb before, I was better than whatever this is now. I'm on my last two bottles of wine. All the weed's done, all the Charlie's finished. Everything's fucking done. I'm opening the second last bottle when my phone starts buzzing.

With every shrill my head rings. Fuck, I'm fucked.

CREAK. I turn my head to the sound, and it's a little cat. I blink a couple more times and stare at it. It's dragging something with it's mouth—

It's an unknown number, I wonder who this could be?

"Hello?" I ask.

"Elmo." It's Dyer. That detective that arrested me time ago. The one that basically wanted me to be his little snitchy-bitch.

Silence.

"Elmo?" He calls.

"What. Do. You. Want."

"Meet me later, around the corner from your place. That alleyway that leads to the main high street," he says.

Is he serious? Yeah, nah. No way I'm leaving my yard. "I can't be bothered for your spy meets. Fuck off."

"Oh Elmo, you'll come. You have to or have you forgotten? You're my bitch." He says, and there it is. The blackmail, extortion— whatever you wanna fucking call it.

"I can't be bothered, bruv."

"See you at 20:00 hours."

"Fuck that," I mutter and down the wine in my paw.

"Excuse me?" He replies. His tone sounds shocked, offended almost.

I'm not his little bitch.

"FUCK. YOU."

"Listen here, you crackhead. You'll show me some respect," he says. I can hear his seriousness from here. I can imagine man looking all stern and all military like. Bruv, what does he think this is? The army. Well, I'm not his fucking solider— that's for sure.

"Pfftt… Well, what do you expect… *from a crackhead?*"

Silence.

I chug some more wine. The bottle's nearly finished. Fuck.

More silence.

I finish the bottle and chuck it on the floor.

THUD.

"Have you got anything for me?" He caved. Not so high and mighty now, is it?

"Nopeeeeeee."

"Elmo— I'm being serious. I know what you did." Shit…

"What did I do?"

"You know what you did."

"I may be high right now— and fucked out of my mind— but do you think I'm fucking stupid? Like I know common sense isn't common— but for fuck's sake. If you had anything on me you wouldn't be asking me this shit. You'd have done it all by now— the whole nine yards. Prison, court—whatever floats your fucking boat." He's fuming. He must be fuming. I just stuck it to him.

Silence.

"Crackhead's still got brain cells." I add and he sniggers through the phone.

"Elmo—" he starts but I cut him off. Fuck that.

I can't be fucking bothered. My head hurts. My body hurts. It all hurts and I've run out of everything.

I don't know what day it is. I don't know how much time has passed, but fuck— it doesn't feel like that long. But looking around me, all I can see for days are empty bottles, cans and baggies.

Fuck.

I… can't even begin to think about—

Ouch, my head—

Gotta stop thinking.

I lay down on the floor. Hopefully this will help my chronic headache… but of course it does fucking nothing. Maybe closing my eyes will help.

So… I close them. Everything's black. Everything's spinning. Nothing's working.

My phone starts ringing again. It's probably Dyer again. Fuck him. Fuck everything, man. It's too much— it's all too fucking much.

RING. RING. RING.

"FUCK OFF! FUCK OFF! FUCK OFF!"

RING. RING. RING.

That's it. I open my eyes and take the bloody thing and throw it into the wall.

SMASH.

Silence.

Finally. Some fucking peace and quiet.

TWENTY

I'm laying down on the floor again. I'm so fucking weak. I drag myself onto the sofa. It's still a piece of shit, from when the police raided my yard way back when. Oh well I don't give a fuck, clearly.

    I'm sitting aren't I?

    Pfftt. I'm laughing.

    MEOW. I look at the cat that came in earlier. I blink slower this time, and take it in. I recognise this cat.

    Why the fuck do I…

    Ahhh HAAA!

    It's the cat that came to mine that day I was fucking about with Oxi and the police burst in. I follow the thing in it's mouth with my eyes—

    —It's one of my satchels.

    The one I had the bomb in. The first one, that I'd lost that day I met Oxi and Jezza. The fucking cat took it— no wonder.

    If anything thank fuck, the cat took it. Probably way better hidden with the little kitty-cat if I'm being honest.

    I reach over and take my last bottle of wine. I open it and chug.

    GULP, GULP, GULP.

I keep going, it's overflowing from my mouth. I can't stop it cumming down all over me. It won't stop. Am I even swallowing enough of it?

I'm drowning in red.

I stand up and I'm struggling.

I feel woozy, like I'm loosing all sense.

STOMP.

What—

THUD.

I'm stumbling forward. I can't stop.

MEOW.

I fell, and onto the cat it seems. I try to push myself up but with no luck. I keep falling back down. When's the last time I ate?

Shit.

My eyes are trying to close but I can't let them…

I reach out and grab the loud cat. It won't shut up.

Tick, tok.

It's fucking with my head.

Tick, tok.

"SHUT UP! SHUT UP! SHUT UP!"

I squeeze harder.

MEOW.

I feel kitty squirming, so I go HARDER.

Tick, tok.

MEOOOOOOOOW.

My eyes burst open, in rage and this time they stay open. I look at my furry red paws—

Tick, tok.

—They're—they're…

Hands?

I can feel the difference of feeling on my skin… that's… *NOT* red fur…

but it's… flesh?

Tick, tok.

What.

The.

Fuck.

Am I seeing things? I let go of the limp cat and bring my hands up in front of me. Human hands…

If— NO.

Tick, tok.

If I'm human… then—

WHO THE FUCK AM I?

Tick, tok.

Was I— Was I just *that* lost in the sauce?

Fuck.

Who am I?

TICK, TOK.

I-If I'm not… Elmo—

Who… am I?

TICK, TOK. TICK, TOK. TICK, TOK.

What the bloody hell is that sound? And that's when I feel it, underneath my belly. My satchel the one the cat brought back—

TICK, TOK. TICK, TOK. TICK, TOK.

Oh no.

TICK, TOK. TICK, TOK. TICK, TOK.

Did I—

TICK, TOK. TICK, TOK. TICK, TOK.

Shit. *Fuck, fuck, fuck.*

What a fuckery… At least I'll really be all red now…

BANG.

THE END.

ACKNOWLEDGMENTS

A massive thank you to my talented friend Phoebe Lochore who made the beautiful illustrations, and who without this book would not have been possible.

I'm forever grateful to my mum for supplying my coffee addiction over the time I was writing this novel.

THROWBACK TO YOU AND THE GIRLIES SNEAKING INTO DOWNING STREET FOR A RIGHT OLD RAVE UP DURING LOCKY D'S

BY

LINDA CARABALI

A meme is a compression of human thoughts; whether they be about the understanding of phrases ("the devil works hard, but Apple works harder" or "it's coming home"), celebrities or public figures, workplaces, countries, current events, on-going / never-ending current events (like Coronavirus, the disappearance of Madeleine McCann, climate change), or just people in their lives, conjoined with captions, images, videos, music or sounds to create a meme; any format of media can potentially carry a meme, so long as one can identify an idea injected from human consciousness within it. More advanced memes, will typically operate with multiple ideas existing adjacent to multiple pockets of realities opening with each, upon identification of the idea(s), to all harmonise simultaneously in one meme; sometimes complex memes can have a family tree as long as a royal bloodline, due to complex memes often becoming cookie-cutters for temporal individual, locational, intimate communication. Aranda, Kuan Wood and Vidokle state, *"the internet does not exist… [as] now it only remains as a blur, a cloud, a friend, a deadline, a redirect or a 404. If it ever existed we couldn't see it. Because it has no shape. It has no face, just this name that describes everything and nothing at the same time."* Much akin to this description of the internet, is the compression of the meme. They adduce, *"We thought there were windows but they're actually mirrors. And in the meantime we are being faced with more and more— not just information, but the world itself"* (Aranda, Kuan Wood and Vidokle, 2015, p. 5). Paul Mason a British commentator and radio personality notes that the functionality of *"memes are a rough and ready democracy— that is, something if you see it working,"* (Metahaven, 2013, p.73) not only are memes a talisman of people's thoughts but also offer insight into the collective attitudes of society within the in-joke. *"Every era, every generation, has to construct and reconstruct its political beliefs, and subsequent visuals, out of the stuff that surrounds it at any given moment"* (Metahaven, 2013, p. 46-47).

Richard Dawkins states, *"[that the computers in which memes live in are human brains]"* (Dawkins, 1976, p. 197). John Cayley, explores time code language in a chapter of *New Media Poetics*, contends *"broadly, [that] codework makes exterior the interior workings of a computer. Code is indeed an archive of symbolic inner workings of the computer. However, not only is it brought to the surface in the writing of new media but it may also function to generate the language displayed on this surface, without itself appearing".* He further explains, the *"distinctions"* between code and text being *"creatively challenged by codework that brings inner workings to an exterior, especially when such work is manifested as a generative cross-infection of text and code-as-text, of language and code-as-language"* (Cayley, 2006, p. 307-308). The actual material code refers to the interior and the text refers to the exterior, yet when codework is in play language forms from a metaphysical interior as it root links their existence to the commonly held world. Similarly, codework within memetics would make the material and metaphysical code the interior and the meme the exterior; making a *"generative cross-infection"* (Cayley, p. 308) of code-as-meme and code-as-language. The compression in memes allows code to be referred to interiorly and exteriorly in any form the meme is. Almost to say, for memes to *"[materialise], a transformation always has to be made"* (Metahaven, 2013, p. 47) to get from interior to exterior.

Compression in memes creates *"a very particular world that has already become part of our consciousness"* as *"it is pegged to its own ability to create meaning, to its ability to refer to something"* (Aranda, Kuan Wood and Vidokle, 2015, p. 5-8). Dawkins talks about *"cultural transmission," that "is analogous to genetic transmission in that, although basically conservative, it can give rise to the form of evolution"* (Dawkins, 1976, p.189). He states *"there are three qualities which define the success of memes: longevity, fecundity and copying-fidelity. Longevity indicates how long a meme can last. Fecundity applies to the appeal of a meme, whether it is catchy and thus likely to spread. Copy-fidelity is about the strength of a meme to withstand mutation in the process of copying and imitation. It determines how much of the original core remains intact when the meme is in transmission"* (Metahaven, 2013, p. 32-33). An example of a meme that has withstood the test of time and had the strength maintain it's *"original core"* (Metahaven, 2013, p. 32-33) is the giant cue-cards scene, from the film *Love Actually* (2003) when Andrew Lincoln's character confesses his unrequited love for Keira Knightley's character using giant cue-cards on Christmas. The scene has become a snapshot template, wherein the text on the cue-cards are written over with whatever you want, you can easily find a meme generator template for this scene on imgflip. Moreover, the scene became so widely known that it has become a cliché vessel for confessions in the romantic comedy genre recently seen in Netflix's *Love Hard* (2021) when Nina Dobrev's character confesses her feelings for Yimmy O. Jang's character. This contrasts with memes to do with politicians which will be forgotten once the politician has lost their relevance in the mainstream media. "It's coming home" has become the stereotypical chant you hear at an England football game from the song Three Lions by David Baddiel, Frank Skinner and The Lightning Seeds. It has been twenty-five years since its release yet it continues to be sung— especially when the England team is actually winning games— because it's not only catchy but carries within it's interior the intimate history of being an England fan. *"The moment the song truly cemented itself into fans' hearts was when it echoed around Wembley at the end of the 1996 clash between England and Scotland"* (Rahman-Jones, 2021). Skinner recounts to Desert Island Discs, England had just won 2-0, they played it over the speaker which followed by the crowd belting out the song. Skinner recalls that as the moment he realised Three Lions had become *"something special"* (Rahman-Jones, 2021)[1].

Figure 1. @TechnicallyRon, Twitter (2020)

---

[1] It is also an example of compression in memes, as "it's coming home" cemented the intimate history of being an England football fan during the 1996 game between England and Scotland. Moreover, it also refers to the fact football started in England, with the patriotic rhetoric that football belongs to the English. This same phrase would later enter a detournement during Euro 2020, when England and Italy played in the 2021 finals. As Italian fans were seen with Italian flags saying, "it's coming home to Rome". See (Tondo, 2021).

Figure 2. Reddit, (2021)

Figure 3. Knowyourmeme, (2019)

"Internet memes
share distinctive features shaped by the unwritten rules

204

of their commonly held world— be it the software used, the online forum inhabited, language spoken or a set of aesthetic preferences… successful memes balance their reference to a commonly held world with an element giving them a strikingly new meaning. The more 'advanced' a meme is, the more its meaning will be implied by the manipulation of the context in which the meme appears" (Metahaven, 2013, p. 39). Through rickrolling Rick Astley's song Never Gonna Give You Up has become a classical meme. What is rickrolling? According to dictionary.com, *"Rickrolling is when you troll someone on the internet by linking to the music video for Rick Astley's 1987 hit song "Never Gonna Give You Up". It is by far the most popular example of bait-and-switch linking"* (Dictionary.com, n.d.) The song is about love yet now people will associate the song to the *"conceptual overhaul"* of being rickrolled where *"all prior sense-making is erased, including the original meaning of Astley's own video"* (Metahaven, 2013, p. 40). Getting rickrolled remains in its new reality, as rickrolling itself has evolved from its origins on 4chan from clicking on an unsuspecting link to display Astley's video. On 30th April 2021 student Minh Duong *"hacked ALL displays in [his] high school district to play Rick Astley"* (Duong, 2021). Although, the premise of clicking a link had disappeared in Duong's rickrolling he exposed 6 schools, with 11,000 enrolled students to the Astley video that day. Yes, the method of delivery had mutated away in this instance, yet at its core it remains the same as its origins in the initial *"conceptual [overhaul's]"* (Metahaven, 2013, p. 40) new reality. *"If a meme is to dominate the attention of a human brain, it must do so at the expense of 'rival' memes"* (Dawkins, 1976, p. 197), it is possible that the rickrolling meme may erase it's link-baiting origins if more imitation's like Duong's hacking start to emerge, as Dawkins explains only time will tell if this new mutation will equate to it's individual success. Metahaven wrongly claims that there is a *"predictable misconception that anything produced following those [distinctive features of the unwritten rules] is bound to be a meme. To not be the case"* (Metahaven, 2013, p. 39). Something can still be a meme without necessarily reaching success through going viral as every meme is made from something else to carry an idea— for example either referring to a notion, thing, person, place, event etc— that already exists in the world. Everything is a distortion of something else, thus for a meme to be understood, ranging from a basic to an advanced meme, it will refer to something already known in the world or else it wouldn't be understood nor have appeal. Bill Drummond and Jimmy Cauty founders of British acid house group, The KLF in their book The Manual, adduce how *"the complete history of the blues is based on a one chord structure, hundreds of thousands of songs using the same three basic chords in the same pattern"* (Drummond and Cauty, 1988, p. 55).

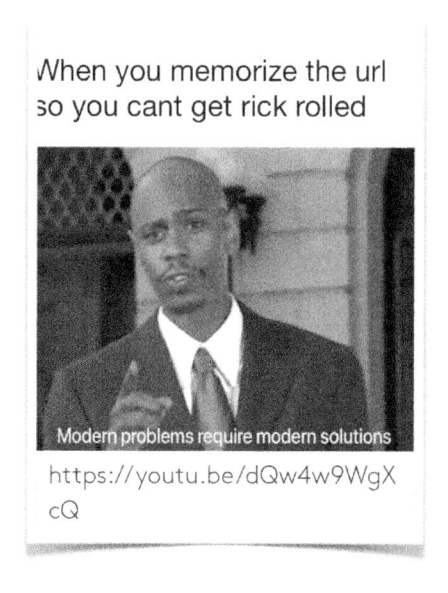

Figure 4. me.me ,(n.d.)

"The task of the artist, in accordance with Plato's theory of art, as surpassing the model of nature

and, by improving on nature, to realise an ideal beauty in his works," (Kris and Kurz, 1979, p. 61) can be seen in an anecdote of how Zeuxis took the most beautiful feature of five girls and pieced them together when doing his painting of Helen. This falls in line with Western notion *"that the artists creates like God, that he is an alter deus. This idea finds its expression in biographies when the artist is elevated to the divino artista—in his heroization"* (Kris and Kurz, 1979, p. 61). On 15th March 2019 two consecutive mass shootings occurred at mosques in a terrorist attack in Christchurch, New Zealand where fifty-one people died and forty were injured. The shooter uploaded a seventy-eight page manifesto and a link to a livestream of the upcoming attack, to 8chan *"one of the main online homes of meme-loving right-wing extremists"* (Romano, 2019). The shooter used memetic language in his manifesto and throughout the terrorist attacks—by having right-wing memes on his guns, live-streaming one of the shootings like it was a first person shooter game when ironically and tragically it was not, saying "subscribe to PewDiePie"[2] during the livestream—he manages to pass off the terrorist attack as a meme, however to his far right white nationalist meme-loving peers, he has immortalised himself through his own heroization. The fact he has created a successful meme through the manifesto and with the forthcoming promise of what was to come, with the livestream link, he positions himself as an *alter deus*. When he carries out the aforementioned attack he solidifies his elevation to the *alter deus* but simultaneously, one could say, the meme led conditioning he went through during his radicalisation (the sources of inspiration the shooter referenced in his manifesto, were manifesto's written by other shooters), was created by masterful artists that are exalted to the *divino artista* status. Coaston states, *"The*

---

[2] PewDiePie, whose full name is Felix Arvid Ulf Kjellberg, is a Swedish Youtuber. He is mainly a web-comedian and gaming channel. He currently (in January 2022) has 111 million subscribers making him the most subscribed individual user on Youtube. He is also the fourth most subscribed channel overall (says Wikipedia). *"The Great Subscriber War, also known as the Subscribe to PewDiePie movement, refers to an ongoing campaign to keep PewDiePie as the most subscribed-to channel on YouTube. The campaign started in 2018 after it was predicted that T-Series, a channel which produces Bollywood music videos, would soon surpass PewDiePie,"* (Knowyourmeme, n.d.).

Christchurch shooter wrote his manifesto with the clear intention of being shared widely after he committed an act of mass murder… historically, terrorist manifestos have never been accurate documentation of either their belief system or the planning that went into their attacks. The main intention of terrorist manifestos is not to help everyday people understand how they become terrorists —it is to create new terrorists." (Coaston, 2019). Deep diving into the memetic rhetoric the New Zealand shooter used, firstly, it references shitposts (defined as *"throwing out red-meat content to readers to distract them or draw them deeper into the same online pits where he himself was radicalised,"* (Coaston, 2019)), memes and public figures. The Youtube personality was called out by the shooter in his livestream of the mass shooting, "Remember lads, Subscribe to PewDiePie." This phrase was started by his fans to protect his YouTube account from being overtaken as the No.1 account with the most subscriptions, with around at the time, 90 million subscribers. Till now, it is unclear if the shooter was really a PewDiePie fan that *so deeply* wanted to support his favourite creator, or if he was using the phrase ironically; as an in-joke and red herring, a nodding to the deeper interior code-as-meme and code-as-language for the subculture and 4chan community, to mock everyone who isn't in the know-how (Dickson, 2019). On why PewDiePie is mixed up in radical meme language, is due to his *"use of 'ironic' anti-semitic or racist humour in his videos that may serve as a gateway for subscribers to start seeking out more overtly extremist content,"* (Dickson, 2019). However, Taylor Lorenz, a staff writer for the *Atlantic* who covers Youtube culture says, *"The problem isn't PewDiePie, the problem is these hard-right fringe communities that are PewDiePie-adjacent"* (Dickson, 2019). Either way by mentioning him, his massive follower base would take a peak, spreading it further, some would find the *"manifesto is a trap"* (Evans, 2019) as it *"is a textbook example of the way right-wing extremists manipulate the media and internet culture"* (Romano, 2019). Around the time on Twitter, people were warning people not to read it, as if one was not used to seeing the interior of memes (and spotting the true meaning / idea the meme carries), they would run the risk of being conditioned, subliminally, by a terrorist whose goal in making public his manifesto, is to create new disciples.

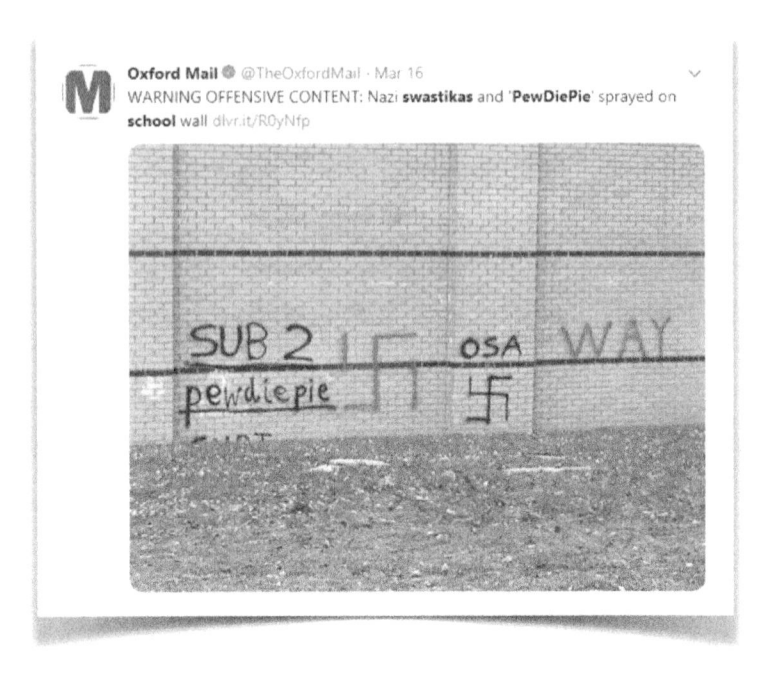

Figure 5. @TheOxfordMail, Twitter (2019)

"Even the motifs are identical—painted animals attract living ones and are taken for real by human beings… the anecdote was often reported in abbreviated form, and thus became a formula for aesthetic judgment" (Kris and Kurz, 1979, p. 65). A meme is *"an element of culture or system of behaviour passed from one individual to another by imitation or other non-genetic means"* (Oxford Languages, n.d.) and the definition given by Dawkins, *"The new replicator, a*

noun that conveys the idea of a unit of cultural transmission, or a unit of imitation" (Dawkins, 1976, p. 192) both surpass the notion of formula as cited above by Kris and Kurz. Although it is true, that through a meme's journey to success, through people does create some sort of *"universal aesthetic judgement,"* (Kris and Kurz, 1979, p. 65) which can easily be visually seen in image, video and sound based internet memes, the truth is, as more people came to understand how to make a meme operate and function to hold idea, it gives way for the evolution of *any media* being able to become a meme. This perhaps would never be on the scale it is today if it was not for the internet making cultural media so accessible.

However, *"The question we must therefore ask is: why was this particular form chosen; why was such confusion between reality and illusion at the very centre of anecdotes?"* (Kris and Kurz, 1979, p. 66) Kris and Kurz pose this question while discussing the imitation of nature and realism in artworks by Giotto and other Renaissance works. They continue to talk about more groups of anecdotes that share *"the same underlying motif… [originating] in classical antiquity… [like that of] Daedalus, the mythical progenitor of Greek art"* (Kris and Kurz, 1979, p. 66). In the Apollodorus tale is as follows; *"one night Hercules is so deceived by the lifelikeness of Daedalus' statue of himself that he throws a stone at it. In one of Euripides' satyr plays an old man, scared out of his wits by the appearance of Hercules, is talked into believing that it was not Hercules but Daedalus's statue of him that he saw.... The form in which these stories have been handed down so closely resembles that of more recent ones, which are scattered throughout biographies of artists, that there can be little doubt about their intimate connection. One is led to assume that the widespread accounts of the public being taken in have their origin in the Daedalus stories cited above... The legends are easily identified as reinterpretations of mythological themes. Originally, possibly as early as the sixth century B.C., Daedalus was regarded as the creator of works which were endowed not just with movement, but even with speech"* (Kris and Kurz, 1979, p. 66-67). Just as different reiterations were passed around of Daedalus' works, almost like a rumour, memes too, carry stories / anecdotes of rumour of their own as during transmission, and mutation happens, things can get distorted. Yet through the anchoring of the anecdote the meme survives with its seed intact, just like in both

Euripides' and Apollodorus' versions the core of the tale survives; that Daedalus can create lifelike statues of a demigod. *"The idea that the artist creates statues that are capable of moving mechanically has a long and venerable history. Daedalus was not the only mythical artist to whom the Greeks ascribed these powers. Homer's Hephaestus was already capable of making mobile figures. He forged not only trinkets and weapons for the gods, but also tripods on golden wheels"* (Kris and Kurz, 1979, p. 68). Interchangeable with memes, there are many times there are a multitude of not only anecdotes, but of cores all interconnected in the same meme-induced pocket of reality. In this case with Hephaestus he is a different seed, yet the anecdote remains the same. However, although every meme comes from the common world, or else it would cease to be understood as a meme, the Greek tales cited above all seem to encase the allure of a magic component. Reality in the sixth century BC, in no way shape or form could have had the technology to create AI operated, human-like robots. However, it begs the question is meme magic real? Or is it just an illusion hidden under fodder? The idea of illusion can clearly be seen in the New Zealand shooter—was he aware of the illusions his mind accepted to be reality, and truth? Well, the answer to that is no— he was not aware because otherwise, he would have not cemented the meme-magic of illusion by committing an act of terrorism.

The idea of a mythical artist also arises *"in Indo-Germanic mythology; the Finnish smith god Ilmarinen also created a golden woman of exceptional beauty and the Lithuanian angels of the art of smithery, Ugniedokas and Ugniegawa, also wrought a living virgin of gold. Reverberations of the theme of a woman created by the mythical artist can still be discerned in the legends of Pygmalion and of the creation of Pandora. Viewed in this context, the anecdote about the deceptive power of works of art, which we found at the beginning of Greek biographies of artists, assumes fresh significance. The gift of creating the illusion of reality, for which it exalts the artist, can be compared to a gift that is distinguishing mark of the mythical artist"* (Kris and Kurz, 1979, p. 69). Talking about illusions merging with reality, for a couple of years now, there is has been a rise in political memes. In the US, they were rising with the left's concerns over Trump being elected— and once he was, well that in itself was a meme because, inside leftist meme communities people had already had been conditioned to see him as a villain so him becoming the President of The Untied States of America was ironic, yet also sinister. This mirrors the state of UK politics through memes, which started gaining popularity after Brexit was voted for, and since 2016 further, has the UK has been politically free-falling into oblivion. The Prime Minister saga; beginning with David Cameron, starts off with him in his resignation speech, *"I held nothing back, I was absolutely clear about my belief that Britain is stronger, safer and better off inside the European Union and I made clear the referendum was about this and this alone—not the future of any single politician including myself. But the British people have made a very clear decision to take a different path and such I think the country requires fresh leadership to take it in this direction. I will do everything I can as prime minister to steady the ship over the coming weeks and months but I do not think it would be right for me to try and be the captain that steers our country to its next destination."* (BBC News, 2016). The meme that arose from Cameron's ashes was his resignation speech with Celine Dion's *My Heart Will Go On* playing in the background, not only was Cameron abandoning his ship after steering it into an iceberg (after he called the referendum in the first place), he then resigns from his post, with everyone else still on the sinking Titanic, Brexit.

Figure 6. Comedy Central UK, Youtube (2017)

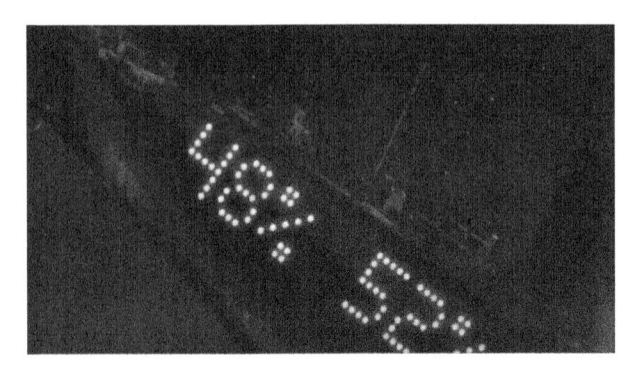

Figure 7. Comedy Central UK, Youtube (2017)

Next up, we had Theresa May. Her infamous answer to, what's the naughtiest thing she'd ever done in an ITV interview, her response? When she and her friends *"used to run through fields of wheat—the farmers weren't too pleased about that,"* (Eleftheriou-Smith, 2017) it generated so many memes that years later and she was still being mocked for it. If you type in, 'Theresa may fields of barley meme' on Google you get 4.4 million results, just to give some scope of how large it was. The next memes, that gained popularity were her dancing in South Africa with the kids, her dancing walk to the podium for a speech, her laughing while looking up in the Houses of Commons, her holding hands with Donald Trump. Moreover, there was an anti-Theresa May meme political protest song by Captain SKA called Liar Liar GE2017, which reached No. 1 in the iTunes UK charts on May 30, 2017, topping Justin Bieber's Despactio at No. 2, and Liam Payne's Strip That Down at No. 3 *"despite receiving no airplay from radio stations because of impartiality guidelines"* (Weaver, 2017).

"[Intro: Theresa May Sample]
"We have a mission to make Britain a country that works, not for the privileged and not for the few, but for

everyone of our citizens. And together we, the Conservative Party, can build a better Britain..."

[Chorus]
She's a liar liar (Oh),
She's a liar liar (No),
You can't trust her,
No, no, no no,
She's a liar liar (Oh),
She's a liar liar (No),
You can't trust her,
No, no, no no,

[Verse 1]
We all know politicians like telling lies,
Big ones, little ones, porky pies,
Saying they're strong and stable won't disguise,
We're still being taken for a ride,
With nurses going hungry,
Schools in decline,
I don't recognise this broken country of mine,
They're having a laugh,
Let's show them the door,
Then cut the rich, not the poor

[Bridge: Theresa May sample]
"I've been very clear that I think we need that period of time, that stability, to be able to deal with the issues that the country is facing. I'm not going to be calling a snap election."

[Chorus]
She's a liar liar (Oh),
She's a liar liar (No),
You can't trust her,
No, no, no no,
She's a liar liar (Oh),
She's a liar liar (No),
You can't trust her,
No, no, no no,

[Verse 2]
I want to have a government that,
Doesn't think that fascism is where it's at,
Cos putting the Mother of all Bombs,
Into tiny hands can go very wrong,
I'm hoping for a future for my child,
Where she can grow, and feel inspired,
Do everything in your power you can,
People rising up is the only plan,

[Bridge 2: Theresa May sample]
"When future generations look back at this time, they will judge us not only by the decision we made, but by what we made of that decision. They will see that we shaped them a brighter future. They will know that we built them a better Britain."

She's a liar liar (Oh),
She's a liar liar (No),
You can't trust her,
No, no, no no,
She's a liar liar (Oh),
She's a liar liar (No),
You can't trust her,
No, no, no no,"
(Genius, 2017).

These lyrics are cleverly written, tapping into the interior code-as-meme and code-as-language by quoting her Brexit catch phrase, *"strong and stable,"* but they hit the ball out of the park in its meme codework when they include a clip in the music video and in the actual audio of the song, of the Prime Minister herself— in her own chart topping anti protest song— *"I've been very clear that I think we need that period of time, that stability, to be able to deal with the issues that the country is facing. I'm not going to be calling a snap election"* (Genius, 2017) her very own words, exalting her own farce. It's almost as if the meme's codework got deeper, as the song is itself is called *Liar Liar GE2017* (which stands for General Election 2017) and also, at the end of the video ends with "On 8 June, Tories out."

Figure 8. @anaveragebrit, Instagram (2019)

Figure 9. @meme.culture.lab, Instagram (2020)

The next PM in the saga, is the current one, Boris Johnson. As like with any British PM since Brexit — there are millions of memes but give or take around ten to fifteen advanced memes that stay for each one after their respective political departures, however, regarding Boris Johnson—there's just *too many* to count with Coronavirus *and* Brexit memes. His memetic codework and history as a public figure goes back to when he was Mayor of London or even before that having— a secret love child with his ~~mistress~~, architect. Boris Johnson is a prime example of the phenomena, of the political in the British meme pool. As his premiership began, the world's opinion was gradually rotting to one of the lowest, Chinese editor of international affairs at *Sanlian Life Week* magazine in Beijing, Liu Ye wrote about how he published a cover story on Brexit, seventy-two hours after the referendum was voted on titled; *"Brexit: are we facing the reversal of globalisation?" That edition sold almost 200,000 copies— even more than [their] report on Donald Trump's presidential win… For the past two or three decades, the US and Britain have been cultural symbols in Chinese people's eyes: the US powerful, rich, enviable; the UK exquisite, elegant. Public intellectuals, especially liberals, all about the British style of constitutionalism, comparing it to [their] Soviet-style totalitarian regime. Students know more about Winston Churchill and Margaret Thatcher than JFK or Bill Clinton. That is real "soft power". But now this image has collapsed. In the Brexit farce, there is no Churchhill or Thatcher, only a dozen mediocre politicians, none of whom want to take responsibility or unite the nation"* (The Guardian, 2019). Sylvie Kauffmann, editorial director and contributor, at *Le Monde* writes watching Emmanuel Macron crushing Le Pen's idea of Frexit *"by proving how incoherent her idea of a French paradise outside the eurozone actually was… has been the only silver lining of the Brexit saga. Watching the long descent of Westminster into something resembling hell has been an exhausting experience. Theresa May's very British resilience was impressive, but [they] ended up pitying her. Nigel Farage's type of was all too familiar to [them; they very] well understood how dangerous he was. Some of [them] once found Boris Johnson funny; [they] long ago stopped laughing… Once, [they] used to hold up British parliamentary life as an example, and watch prime minister's questions in the House of Commons with envy: for [them], accustomed to semi-monarchical presidents of the Republic, this was the very Rolls-Royce of liberal democracy. Now that Rolls-Royce looks more like a dodgem"* (The Guardian, 2019). Khuê Pham, staff writer at German magazine *Zeit* wrote he learned about their *"blindspots as reporters [as he] saw parallels to Brexit not just in Donald Trump's election victory later that year, but also in the rise of Alternative für Deutschland at the 2017 elections in Germany… For [their] readers at Die Ziet, Boris Johnson is by far the most intriguing character in the Brexit drama. He makes them come out in a rash— it's as if they are allergic to him. They feel he has been disdainful towards Europeans, treating Europe as a big joke. That view will stick around even as prime minister — quoting witty lines in Latin won't change that…Britain's soft power has already started to diminish. Caught up in Brexit, the UK government doesn't have the bandwidth to play a role in European politics any more"* (The Guardian, 2019). Nobuyuki Suzuki, media and entertainment news editor, the *Tokyo Shimbun* newspaper stated, *"The Japanese have always seen Britain as a gentle, stable country, but that has changed, first because of Brexit and now because of the rise of Boris Johnson. Johnson doesn't fit the stereotype of an English gentleman. He reminds a lot of people in Japan of Donald Trump, both physically and in terms of his political style. Johnson looks a little wild, and he speaks his mind… what he says about politics doesn't really matter to the Japanese… instead [they] are intrigued by the fact he doesn't speak or behave like a conventional politician"* (The Guardian, 2019). Mihir Sharma, author, *Bloomberg* columnist, and senior fellow at the *Observer Research Foundation*, New Delhi voices *"observing the saga unfold from afar, is high comedy: a political class that is trapped by its own promises and lies into delivering the undeliverable and which is now losing all credibility as a consequence. It's been strange to watch the incredible arrogance on display in England (not Britain), which reveals itself in this belief that they will somehow be a desirable location or partner for other countries once they leave Europe. Such a giant and inexplicable act of self harm would be sad if it happened to a country less sure of itself, but when it happens to England, it is assuming as well. Britain confuses its standing with that of London. London is a great global city. Britain is a small European country with ideas above its station… It seems to [him] that too many people in London seem to believe, deep down that Brexit won't happen. They don't seem to realise they are now strangers in their own country"* (The Guardian, 2019). Alexey Venediktov, editor-in-chief, *Echo of Moscow* radio station expresses, *"The British leadership is now seen as the most actively hostile European government to Russia [(due to the Skripal case)]. Unfortunately, the view of Boris Johnson in the leadership is quite negative. They don't think he is serious. They think he's a clown. And second, they think he has little support in his party and his country. So he's temporary… we'll wait for the new leader"* (The Guardian, 2019). The world rhetoric that the UK was rotting, functions as the interior code for meme codework; code-as-meme, conjoined with the phenomena of Boris Johnson being a walking political meme creating the meme-as-language which together formulates the exterior code of making Great Britain, a meme; a country whose news and politics merely serves as an in-joke for entertainment purposes, much like reality TV shows like *Love Island, The Only Way is Essex* and other so-called 'trash' TV. The international foreign powers, as well as foreign opinion, who is outside of Great Britain (the meme) are the ones who are being entertained. However, the truth is, the UK is a sovereign nation— which means what happens regarding Johnson, May, Cameron and Brexit is in fact occurring at its highest levels of government, making it reality. However, this reality has been over-run by millions of basic-level memes relating to the individuals at power and never-ending political failings, each and every one their own meme pools, and separate pockets of realities. Thus, creating a meme tsunami carrying the idea that the UK is unserious and the end of a never-ending butt-joke, which in-turn has the desensitised British news as *actual* news, during the time of Brexit, there was a merging between illusion and reality occurring, because the UK is real, yet everything that was being reported seemed more and more unrealistic, which misbalanced the perception of the meme illusion (it's pocket of reality), therefore, illusion and reality became one. When this happened, it elevated foreign international powers as well foreign media and opinion to the *artista divino*, moreover since this meme is built on the unification of illusion and reality, for their elevation to the *artista divino*, the UK, through their own leaders, would have to also cement themselves as the *alter deus*, the creators of the meme magic itself as they are the core seeds to all memes and all memes pools from them, that pertain to the fall of grace of the UK. Ironically, because they are the ones driving themselves off a cliff and aiding the meme illusion to cement, oxymoronically would also make them the *artista divino* and *alter deus* because the memes that have merged illusion and reality would never have existed if the UK had not self-harmed.

> **Sophie Deck the Halls**
> @SophLouiseHall
>
> "Hello I am the police officer investigating the No 10 Christmas party"

Figure 10. @madeinpoortaste, Instagram (2021)

Günter Berghaus discusses anarchist rebellion and facist reaction during 1909-1944 in his book, Futurism and Politics. He says, *"Marinetti believed that theatre as a form of "cultural combat" would lead the artists out of their ivory towers and give them a chance "to participate, like workers or soldiers, in the battle for world progress,""* (Berghaus, 1996, p. 73). This is notion is keenly proven through reactionary activist memes, that often convey ideas of outrage, a good example of this is the Black Lives Matter movement that sparked a new era of riots and protest across the world. Kris and Kurz when talking about portraiture and *"the belief in the identity of portrait and the portrayed— which the French philosopher Charles Lalo cleverly termed the first aesthetic theory of mankind— not only... associated with the origin of representational art, but also governed the formation of legends concerned with the beginning of art"* (Kris and Kurz, 1979, p. 74). They mention the legends of the lines being drawn around a person's shadow, to imply the shadow is a potential picture, thus creating portraiture. Furthermore, two more motifs with this same base code are mentioned but mutated and evolved into the origins of sculpture. Boutades, a Sicyounian potter's daughter painted the outline of her departing beloved on a wall and her father filled the gap, thus erecting the first sculpture. The second is rooted in Tibetan and Mongolian legends about the origin of the Buddha image. An artist tried and failed to do his portrait so he had his shadow traced on a wall and filled. (Kris and Kurz, 1979, p. 74) The origins of portraiture act as code-as-meme for the interior as, the origins of sculpture act as code-as-language to create meme codework for *"the second type of legend about origins of art is based on the belief that the image is a replacement of a dead person"* (Kris and Kurz, 1979, p. 75). This idea resonates with image and moving image, digital or analogue, that came to largely replace painting as a means to record and document life, making art a more abstract concept, causing the art world to re-define what explicitly art is / functions for in society. Can some forms of memes be considered art? Considering that Kirchner *"in 1916 he wrote from Köruigstein im Taunus, where he had gone in hope of a cure [(after his creative spirit left when World War I broke out) that]... the heaviest burden of all is the pressure of the war and the increasing superficiality... Swollen, I stagger to work, but all my work is in vain and the mediocre is tearing everything down in its onslaught. I'm now like the whores I used to paint, Washed out, gone next time,"* (Dube, 1979, p. 46). Unlike Kirchner's description of the pressures of making art in bleak social times, internet memes have none, hence a more natural and raw expression of communication. Perhaps the very fact memes, particularly internet memes, are not officially accepted in the mainstream as a form of art is to protect the unconscious low-pressure compulsive purpose to create memes. Thus, keeping the freedom of idea and democracy alive within the in-joke, whether you partake or not (if anything by rejecting the meme as art, you further cement the meme's illusions in society. Moreover, if memes were accepted as a mainstream form of art it would cease to have the same communicative function it has today). *"Mystery speaking through mysteries. Isn't that meaning? Isn't that the conscious or unconscious purpose of the compulsive urge to create? Kandinsky had asked in 1910"* (Dube, 1979, p. 112). On Max Beckmann, *"Curt Glaser wrote in 1924: "Beckmann is one of those artists who are compelled to communicate. He is an "Expressionist," not by virtue of his form, but by virtue of his inner compulsion,"* (Dube, 1979, p.162) and thus, the term expressionist meme arrives. George Floyd's death being recorded and shared around social media, is what caused the Black Lives Matter movement to gain worldwide cross-racial traction last summer. "I can't breathe," would become a man's dying words, but in doing so would impact hundreds, upon thousands of people. His last words because a universal chant at protests all around the world. People standing up against police brutality and racism. Many people would not like the video of his death being called a meme—because there surrounds a common misconception in the mainstream outside of the internet meme communities that memes are nothing more than humours and unserious— yet it is a meme, just as the massacre at Christchurch, New Zealand is (the difference is that, the shooter was aware the whole event would be a meme, as the *alter deus*). Arguably Darnella Frazier could be the *alter deus* as she recorded his death then posted it on social media, making George Floyd himself an *artista divino* by dying. However, although he did not want to die —his lack of intention arguably can revoke his status as *artista divino*, however, he did in fact die which cannot change— thus, elevating the heroization of Frazier. Another question is, now that meme illusion and reality can merge, by the existence of the UK being a meme, can the meme and art merge? Can information and data be considered art? The death of George Floyd and the livestream of a massacre both became memes, if one would see them on Instagram or Facebook in the meta-verse a pop-up would appear saying the clips are for 'educational purposes,' yet if news can now be considered a meme are you learning an illusion or is reality the illusion? Either way can be argued, Christchurch would be the illusion of a white nationalist viewpoint and BLM would be showing what police brutality and being black is really like. Where is the line? But should there be one, if it is educational, and more so if a line is drawn it will seal off illusions and realities where they are presently. Which would be bad for the UK for example, as the meme illusion, would become something they can never change— which for a change of narrative would require the same meme tools to infect the existing meme pools— but that cannot happen until the *alter deus* and *artista divino*— the UK leaders do something the meme pools deem worthy, as memes *"[replace] the messy exchange on a blog, which in turn replaced the in-depth thinking that exists in books, effectively recreating the [social media] user as a judge... this loop"* (Rich, 2015, p. 160-161) could potentially continue forever as memes have all the tools to survive and mutate, as Dawkins calls them, "selfish genes" which have no end.

Figure 11. @wallofcomdey, Instagram (2021)

PewDiePie was forced to 'end' the Subscribe to PewDiePie meme after the Christchurch shooting as he was shocked and did not want him or his community dragged into the 4chan, white nationalist rhetoric surrounding the New Zealand shooter. *"His message comes just after the accused San Diego synagogue shooter, John Earnest, apparently published a manifesto online in which he also referenced PewDiePie"* (Flynn, 2019). To effectively kill the meme illusions created by the terrorists, PewDiePie had to address and express his distain and effectively ask his fans to stop spreading the movement (that before Christchurch had been ongoing for seven months), so that eventually it would die out and be overwritten by some other viral narrative. During 2021, Netflix's *Squid Game* (2021) became its most watched show worldwide once it aired, dominating No.1 on UK Netflix and in 90 other countries having racked up 111 million users watching it in the first 28 days of release. The Korean show is about people who have hit rock bottom being mysteriously invited to and participating in a thriller-dystopian-like, play or be killed type game for a life-changing amount of money (Sharman, 2021). The show garnered such a massive following, that people started posting memes online about the show as people thought it was a clever and insightful way to show how greed and capitalism led to a lack of human compassion, as the game was quite literally play and be killed, risk it all—including your life— for a mere, not even certainty of earning money. There could only be one winner, as the episodes progressed, more players died, and each episode the moral slippage in the characters was coming closer to a cold savagery. This was seen in the progress of the main character, played by Lee Jung-Jae as he saw the characters around him turn into ruthless killers to survive.

    Not only were there Squid Game memes about it being a reflection of capitalism and humanity in society— but the show itself is a meme. The comparisons being so close to reality that, even North Korea has weighted in (even though it is illegal to watch South Korean shows there), *"a North Korean propaganda website, opined that Squid Game reflects the "sad reality of the beastly South Korean society", where "corruption and immoral scoundrels are commonplace"…It added that [Squid Game] illuminates "the reality of living in a world where people are judged by only money""* (Mahdawi, 2021). This elevates the show and its creator to the *artista divino,* acting as the exterior code-as-meme, as it is not only the seed of all its memes but is also the reason they exist. One popular meme, is the real-life Squid Games inspired by the show, where participants win money. However, not all are wholesome and legit. Police in London issued warnings over a Squid Game inspired free fight-for-all dodgeball game where the winner would win £10,000, and the eliminated players would get shot in the face with a BB gun. This specific one, and many others like it required participation fees (McCallig, 2021). Memes where they would attempt to replicate the show and make money, cement Capitalism as the *alter deus,* acting as the interior code-as-language, as it is the core origins of the show and, comes back around full circle like a boomerang with Netflix's monetary success, as well as with people looking to profit from making real-life games. Moreover, once it achieves the status of *alter deus* it simultaneously also becomes the *artista divino* as Capitalism drives Capitalism. Netflix would never have invested millions into the budget for a low return, and they cashed out. People started wondering when season 2 would come out, yet the creator says he has no plans for a season 2 at the moment.

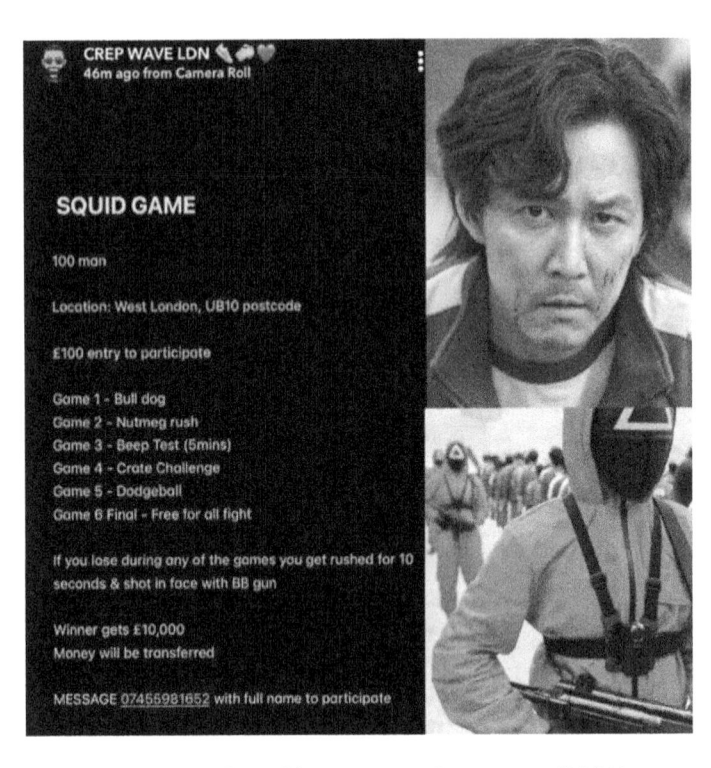

Figure 12. @Fxshionconcept, Instagram (2021)

 In the last episode the viewer finds out the purpose of the Squid Games for the VIP hosts; that they bet on people's lives in the games, like they were avatars in a video game. They had become so monotone and bored of life, that having front row seats and passive participation in a reality TV show type-of-way[3] to a Battle-Royale inspired game to the death was the only way to give them entertainment and excitement. Although Squid Game is fiction, there seems to be a direct link to it's interior code-as-language, capitalism and people in power playing people like chess pieces on a board for fun. This can be seen in recent Conservative party scandals involving the alleged multiple Christmas parties that were held at No. 10 Downing Street last year when London was in tier 4 Coronavirus restrictions. Last year, the restrictions were so strict people had to cancel their Christmas plans, leave loved ones who weren't in their household support bubble alone and attend work, school, marriages and funerals online through Zoom. Johnson denied all knowledge of a Christmas party occurring at No.10 when the news broke in the first week of December 2021, yet *"Allegra Stratton, Johnson's former press secretary, was filmed laughing*

---

[3] Refers to shows like *Love Island, I'm a Celebrity Get Me Out of Here, Strictly Come Dancing, X Factor* etc… where audiences watching can call in or vote to nominate contestants, yet the participation is passive enough to allow for the contestants to change an audience's absolute decision, hence why it is passive participation. For example, on *Love Island* audiences may vote to pair up a contestant to go on a date with a new islander, but the contestants may not actually have romantic chemistry, hence an unsuccessful date.

about it anyway in a video that was leaked to ITV News. Which was somewhat unfortunate for all those that insisted it never took place. Obviously Stratton had to resign from her current job, for laughing about a party that didn't happen" (Silverman, 2021).

As the weeks went on into January more news about the Christmas parties emerged, to the point a meme clip of Boris dancing with a lightsaber went viral, insinuating it was taken at the 2021 Christmas party—but the clip is actually from a Christmas party in 2013 when Johnson was Mayor of London. This spurned on more reactionary memes across the internet. People have become so desensitised to the news and are so accustomed with Boris Johnson as a meme, that it doesn't matter what the truth is anymore. Every little thing to do with him and the Conservative party aides the interior code-as-language that reality has become nonsense, and by this point today, January 2022 after the Coronavirus pandemic illusion and reality merged, creating the magic of meme illusion becoming the new reality and thus, people are more desensitised to the news now more than ever before. During the pandemic there were more times that the government further added to this particular meme illusion that has led to what it is now. During March 2020, CNN aired a news-segment of a viral meme that compared a phrase in one of Boris Johnsons' Coronavirus announcements, *"many more families are going to lose loved ones before their time,"* to *Shrek*'s Lord Faquaad speech when he was trying to get the people go and recuse Fiona instead of himself, *"some of you may die but it's a sacrifice I'm willing to make"* (Dosani, 2020). This meme adds to the rhetoric that the government doesn't care about anyone but themselves and that they take people for fools; that it's one rule for them and another for everyone else. The Matt Hancock meme scandal that made him lose his job as Secretary of State for Health furthers this. He was the politician in charge of health during the COVID-19 lockdowns, and advised the country to have 2 meter social distancing among other things, to prevent people catching Coronavirus yet a CCTV snapshot leaked of him snogging Gina Coladangelo, exposing their affair and the fact they broke the COVID related restrictions in place at the time, as they are both married to other people, thus not in the same household bubble.

Figure 13. @Ladbible, Instagram (2021)

Through the constant downward spiral the news had turned into during the 2020 Coronavirus pandemic, meme illusions cemented themselves within current events, making the news seem like it was nonsense, like it was not possible that the earth was on global lockdown. That there was a deadly virus spreading, which no one had a cure to— from March 2020 the news was starting to sound like the plot to a Hollywood blockbuster. There were constant memes comparing the rapidly updating Coronavirus government announcements made by Johnson, a popular one in particular was the caption, 'what in the hunger games is this?'. During the pandemic it gave rise to Futurist memes, not to be mistaken for *"belonging or relating to futurism, a way of thinking in the arts that started in the early 20th century and tried to express through a range of art forms the characteristics and images of the modern age, such as machines, speed, movement and power,"* but rather *"a person who makes statements about what will happen in the future based on their studies and knowledge."* (Cambridge Dictionary, n.d.). The Coronavirus pandemic successfully cemented the meme codework in regard to the government being useless and inept, that it has merged reality and illusion, into a new meme reality. Simultaneously, once this collectively occurred throughout the political meme codework, it exposed the illusion of both the meme and reality from which the new post-coronavirus reality emerged from, thus leaving a depression and sad outlook on what life is. Not only has media essentially become completely untrustworthy, but the very farce of democracy in the UK has even begun to surface with people being distracted by Conservative party scandals, people become unaware of bills passing through parliament. This meme codework has become so powerful it has really and truly desensitised people to the media—however, the flip side of that, is the fact they are only seeing the smoke and mirrors, the week the Christmas party scandal broke the media was solely reporting on that, and yet the government passed the Nationality and Borders Bill the very same week— when people got wind of it and started to protest the bill it was already too late as it was only reported on by mainstream media after it had passed and protests began.

Figure 14. @lockdown.memes, Instagram (2020)

This meme codework, has created a rhetoric that the people in power are clowns and fools, however, as *alter deus* and *artista divino* they have created a smoke and mirror which allows them to do what they like behind closed doors, just as *"internet memes don't do any mediation at all, and are all about the inessential taking some kind of center-stage,"* (Metahaven, 2013, p. 72) they too have made the country's media inessential making finding real news, harder and fake news, easier. How is it possible to break down the very construct of a country and diminish it to being a meme? (It gives rise to another question; of complete erasure of reality— is the country even real? Or is the country just an idea? This type of meme phenomena is what led to the meme in which people questioned if Australia is a real country.[4]) Having a Conservative government during two critical watershed time periods, that's what. Brexit and Coronavirus; were key times for this political meme phenomena to occur, the later only cementing how bleak things really are. Futurist memes have become somewhat of an escapism to current affairs / situations since the pandemic. However, before the Pandemic there were futurist memes that were not focused on the theme of escaping this new-corona-age-reality, like when *The*

---

[4] See, (Ball, 2018) and (Knowyourmeme, 2017).

Simpsons 'predicted the future' time and time again; Trump being President, the Coronavirus pandemic, Astroworld[5], faulty voting machines etc… (McCluskey, 2020).

DSG suggests that the Goatse (an image of a man stretching his rectum) is Industrial Sabotage and is *"in reality a return of Jan van Toorn's "dialogic image." Goaste emerged in the same way Rickrolling did… in turn then, Van Toorn's work would be a pre-interactive form of "linkbaiting"; in the absence of links to click on, the designer already combined different target images into a single collage. Was Van Toorn indeed Rickrolling his audience, avant le lettre? In a dialogic image, says DSG, "the design presents multiple conflicting messages, with a view to forcing a demystified, critical reading from its audience."* (Metahaven, 2013, p. 69). This in regard to memetics, displays how in meme codework; interior code-as-language, has become the true form of expression. As Van Toorn, whether consciously or

---

[5] Referring to Travis Scott's Astroworld album's cover art in conjunction with the incident at Astroworld festival November 5, 2021 with 10 fatalities. Memes surfaced about the deaths being *"Satanic"* rituals. See, (Hurley, 2021).

unconsciously was pre-computer click-baiting, memes on the other hand, can unconsciously float around in the mainstream, as reality and illusion merging have paved a way for memes to exist in the form of pure idea in the mainstream —thus making them harder for people unfamiliar with memetic rhetoric to detect—and developing as an internet meme could be replicated in different ways over time, only in thought. Whether one is clued into the in-joke or not, all are equally conditioned subtlety through the conditioning because memes are selfish and they will never stop replicating, unless you put an end to them like PewDiePie did. The subtlety is what is hidden here, in the long-term effects of the manipulation of reality through illusion. From the extreme behaviours; from Trump loyalists storming the Capitol building in the beginning of 2021, to people on TikTok believing Travis Scott sacrificed his fans to Satan during the Astroworld tragedy and to terrorists using meme language as a red herring to radicalise new disciples— these are a few examples of just how far memes can go to alter reality, not all memes should be taken lightly— gradually they start to shape your environment, (the Christchurch shooter should be example enough to demonstrate how meme rhetoric can transform in the wrong hands over time, and just how dangerous the effects of it's subliminal messaging is /or can be). These examples demonstrate how rational thinking, and common logic have gone out the window and illuminate how memetic rhetoric is gradually desensitising moralities, ethics and values that uphold society into an era of dark humour, fake news and *"an age of disenchantment with political institutions"* (Metahaven, 2013, p. 72).

Figure 15. @meme_0_mat, Instagram (2020)

Bibliography

McCluskey, M. (2020) *17 Times The Simpsons Accurately Predicted the Future.* Available at: https://time.com/4667462/simpsons-predictions-donald-trump-lady-gaga/ (Accessed: 24 January 2022).

Ball, J. (2018) *Australia doesn't exist! And other bizarre geographic conspiracies that won't go away.* Available at: https://www.theguardian.com/technology/shortcuts/2018/apr/15/australia-doesnt-exist-and-other-bizarre-geographic-conspiracies-that-wont-go-away (Accessed: 19 April 2022).

Cambridge Dictionary (n.d.) Meaning of futurist in English. Avaliable at: https://dictionary.cambridge.org/dictionary/english/futurist (Accessed: 24 January 2022).

Sales, D. (2022) *'It was a work event in the basement actually': Footage of Boris Johnson disco dancing becomes massive online hit as flood of memes over Downing Street parties scandal continues.* Available at: https://www.dailymail.co.uk/news/article-10402171/It-work-event-basement-actually-Footage-Boris-Johnson-disco-dancing-hit.html (Accessed: 24 January 2022).

Sharman, L. (2021) *Squid Game breaks Netflix record with 111 million users watching.* Available at: https://www.standard.co.uk/news/uk/squid-game-netflix-bridgertonrecord-views-b960317.html?amp (Accessed: 24 January 2022).

Mahdawi, A. (2021) *Netflix's Squid Game savagely satirises our money-obsessed society- but it's capitalism that is the real winner.* Available at: https://www.theguardian.com/commentisfree/2021/oct/20/netflix-squid-game-savagely-satirises-our-money-obsessed-society-but-capitalism-is-the-real-winner (Accessed: 24 January 2022).

Rich, J. (2015) 'Facebook: A Court of Ignorant, Cruel Judges', in e-flux journal, *The Internet Does Not Exist*. Berlin: Sternberg Press, pp. 150-161.

Aranda, J., Kuan Wood, B. and Vidokle, A. (2015) 'Introduction', in e-flux journal, *The Internet Does Not Exist*. Berlin: Sternberg Press, pp. 5-9.

Cayley, J. (2006) 'Time Code Language: New Media Poetics and Programmed Signification', in Morris, A. and Swiss, T. (eds.) *New Media Poetics*. Cambridge, Massachusetts: The MIT Press, pp. 307-333.

Dawkins, R. (1976) *The Selfish Gene.* Oxford: Oxford University Press.

Metahaven (2013) *Can Jokes Bring Down Governments?*. Moscow: Strelka Press.

Love Actually (2003) Directed by Curtis, R. [Film]. StudioCanal, France. Universal Pictures, USA.

Love Hard (2021) Directed by Jimenez, H. [Film]. Worldwide, Netflix.

Squid Game (2021) Netflix, 17 September 2021.

Surviving R. Kelly (2019) Netflix, 3 January 2019.

Evans, G. (2021) *A brief history of the 'It's Coming Home' meme and why England fans still sing it.* Available at: https://www.indy100.com/sport/england-its-coming-home-meme-b1872875 (Accessed: 6 January 2022).

Rahman-Jones, I. (2021) *It's coming home: How Three Lions became the definitive England song.* Available at: https://www.bbc.co.uk/news/newsbeat-44711564 (Accessed: 6 January 2022).

Knowyourmeme (2017) *Australia Is Not Real.* Available at: https://knowyourmeme.com/memes/australia-is-not-real (Accessed: 19 April 2022).

Imgflip (n.d.) *Love Actually sign Meme Generator.* Available at: https://imgflip.com/memegenerator/27970565/love-actually-sign (Accessed: 6 January 2022).

Dictionary (2022) *Slang Dictionary; Rickrolling.* Available at: https://www.dictionary.com/e/slang/rickrolling/ (Accessed: 6 January 2022).

Duong, M. (2021) *How I hacked ALL displays in my high school district to play Rick Astley.* Available at: https://thenextweb.com/news/how-i-hacked-high-school-rick-astley-rickrolling-syndication (Accessed: 6 January 2022).

Coaston, J. (2019) *The New Zealand shooter's manifesto shows how white nationalist rhetoric spreads.* Available at: https://www.vox.com/identities/2019/3/15/18267163/new-zealand-shooting-christchurch-white-nationalism-racism-language (Accessed: 6 January 2022).

Romano, A. (2019) *How the Christchurch shooter used memes to spread hate.* Available at: https://www.vox.com/culture/2019/3/16/18266930/christchurch-shooter-manifesto-memes-subscribe-to-pewdiepie (Accessed: 6 January 2022).

Dickson, E. J. (2019) *Why Did the Christchurch Shooter Name-Drop YouTube Phenom PewDiePie?.* Available at: https://www.rollingstone.com/culture/culture-news/pewdiepie-new-zealand-mosque-shooting-youtube-808633/ (Accessed: 6 January 2022).

Flynn, M. (2019) *'I didn't want hate to win': PewDiePie ends 'subscribe' meme after Christchurch shooter's shout-out.* Available at: https://www.washingtonpost.com/nation/2019/04/29/i-didnt-want-hate-win-pewdiepie-ends-subscribe-meme-after-christchurch-shooters-shout-out/ (Accessed: 6 January 2022).

Gant, J. (2021) *'His advisors really are muppets!' Boris Johnson is mocked over Kermit the Frog reference in climate change speech to the UN after he told delegates 'It IS easy to be green'.* Available at: https://www.dailymail.co.uk/news/article-10020771/Boris-Johnson-mocked-Kermit-Frog-reference-climate-speech-UN.html (Accessed: 6 January 2022).

Drummond, B. and Cauty, J. (1988) *The Manual.* London: Ellipsis.

Kris, E. and Kruz, O. (1979) *Legend, Myth & Magic In The Image Of The Artist.* London: Yale University Press.

Oxford Languages (n.d.) *Meme defintion.* Available at: https://www.google.com/search?q=meme+definition&oq=meme+de&aqs=chrome.1.69i57j0i5

12l8j46i512.6771j0j7&sourceid=chrome&ie=UTF-8 (Accessed: 6 January 2022).

Silverman, R. (2021) *Welcome to the meme party: how the internet skewered the No 10 'non-event'*. Available at: https://www.telegraph.co.uk/news/2021/12/10/welcome-meme-party-internet-skewered-no-10-non-event/ (Accessed: 6 January 2022).

Pyman, T. (2021) *Line of Duty creator takes aim at Boris after PM dons police uniform for drugs bust in Merseyside - triggering wave of ridicule over his 'Brian Harvey' beanie.* Available at: https://www.dailymail.co.uk/news/article-10284255/Line-Duty-creator-takes-aim-Boris-PM-dons-police-uniform-drugs-bust-Merseyside.html (Accessed: 6 January 2022).

McKenna, K. (2021) Boris Johnson: *Could he be the worst PM in Britain's history?* Available at: https://www.heraldscotland.com/politics/19770356.boris-johnson-worst-pm-britains-history/ (Accessed: 6 January 2022).

BBC News (2016) *Brexit: David Cameron's resignation statement in full.* Available at: https://www.bbc.co.uk/news/uk-politics-eu-referendum-36619446 (Accessed: 6 January 2022).

BBC News (2018) *Theresa May dances with school children during her South Africa visit.* Available at: https://twitter.com/BBCNews/status/1034372821529571328?ref_src=twsrc%5Etfw%7Ctwcamp%5Etweetembed%7Ctwterm%5E1034377091276595200%7Ctwgr%5E%7Ctwcon%5Es3_&ref_url=https%3A%2F%2Fd-24850531191129625445.ampproject.net%2F2111242025001%2Fframe.html (Accessed: 6 January 2022).

Evans, G. (2019) *Theresa May has resigned but at least she has left us with memes.* Available at: https://www.indy100.com/news/theresa-may-resigs-prime-minister-tory-memes-brexit-8928401 (Accessed: 6 January 2022).

The Daily Edge (2017) *The best memes from when Theresa May admitted the naughtiest thing that she has ever done.* Available at: https://www.dailyedge.ie/theresa-may-wheat-memes-3434924-Jun2017/ (Accessed: 6 January 2022).

Mills, J. (2019) *Theresa May really regrets that 'field of wheat' confession.* Available at: https://metro.co.uk/2019/07/17/theresa-may-really-regrets-field-wheat-confession-10395636/ (Accessed: 6 January 2022).

Weaver, M. (2017) *'She's a liar, liar': anti-Theresa May song heads to top of charts.* Available at: https://www.theguardian.com/politics/2017/may/31/liar-liar-anti-theresa-may-song-heads-to-top-of-charts (Accessed: 6 January 2022).

Captain SKA (2017) Liar Liar GE2017. Available at: https://youtu.be/HxN1STgQXW8 (Accessed: 6 January 2022).

The Guardian (2019) *'Something resembling hell': how does the rest of the world view the UK?*. Available at: https://www.theguardian.com/politics/2019/aug/04/how-does-the-rest-of-the-world-currently-view-the-uk-brexit-boris-johnson (Accessed: 7 January 2022).

Nevett, J. (2020) *George Floyd: The personal cost of filming police brutality.* Available at: https://www.bbc.co.uk/news/world-us-canada-52942519 (Accessed: 7 January 2022).

Genius (2017) *Liar Liar GE2017 Lyrics.* Available at: https://genius.com/Captain-ska-liar-liar-ge2017-lyrics (Accessed: 24 January 2022).

PewDiePie (n.d.) Ending the Subscribe to Pewdiepie Meme. Available at: https://www.youtube.com/watch?v=Ah5MYGQBYRo (Accessed: 6 January 2022).

Dube, W.-D. (1979) *The Expressionists.* London: Thames and Hudson.

Jung, C.-G., Von Franz, M.-L., Henderson, J. L., Jaffé, A. and Jacobi, J. (1964) *Man and His Symbols.* New York: Dell Publishing.

Propp, V (1968) *Morphology of the Folktale.* Austin: University of Texas Press.

Bernstein, C. (1973) *'The Fake As More'* in Battcock, G. *Idea Art.* New York: E.P Dutton & Co., Inc., pp. 41-45.

Kaminsky, J. (1962) *Hegel on Art.* New York: The Comet Press.

Berghaus, G. (1996) *Futurism and Politics.* New York: Berghahn Books.

Berger, J., Blomberg, S., Fox, C., Dibb, M. and Hollis, R. (1972) *Ways of Seeing.* London: Penguin Books.

Dosani, R. (2020) *CNN compares Boris Johnson to Shrek's Lord Farquaad in coronavirus bulletin.* Available at: https://metro.co.uk/2020/03/17/boris-johnsons-coronavirus-speech-compared-lord-farquaad-shrek-no-one-can-cope-12414181/ (Accessed: 5 January 2022).

Times of India (2021) *Social Humour: #CivilWar memes go viral as Trump loyalists lay siege to Capitol Hill.* Available at:

https://timesofindia.indiatimes.com/humour/social-humour/
social-humour-civilwar-memes-go-viral-as-trump-loyalists-
lay-siege-to-capitol-hill/articleshow/80144505.cms
(Accessed: 5 January 2022).

News One (2019) *17 R. Kelly Memes Destroying His Tragic Interview With Gayle King.* Available at: https://newsone.com/playlist/r-kelly-memes/item/15 (Accessed: 5 January 2022).

Wade, B. (2021) *Becoming a meme: Tessica Brown on becoming Gorilla Glue Woman.* Available at: https://filmdaily.co/memes/tessica-brown/ (Accessed: 5 January 2022).

Hurley, B. (2021) *Astroworld: How bogus 'satanic panic' conspiracy theorists are hijacking a senseless tragedy.* Available at: https://www.independent.co.uk/news/world/americas/astroworld-satanic-conspiracies-travis-scott-b1955165.html (Accessed: 5 January 2022).

McCallig, E. (2021) *Squid Game has inspired real-life spin-offs, but not all of them are legit.* Available at: https://www.indy100.com/news/squid-game-real-life-spin-offs-b1936116 (Accessed: 5 January 2022).

Cooper, G. F (2021) *England storms into Euro 2020 final, memes say it's coming home.* Available at: https://

www.cnet.com/google-amp/news/england-storms-into-euro-2020-final-memes-say-its-coming-home/ (Accessed: 5 January 2022).

Evans, G. (2021) *Ryanair has been trolling Boris Johnson and the government with memes for more than a week.* Available at: https://www.google.co.uk/amp/s/www.indy100.com/news/ryanair-boris-johnson-government-memes-b1977185%3famp (Accessed: 6 January 2022).

Eleftheriou-Smith, L.-M. (2017) *Theresa May reveals naughtiest things she has ever done was 'running through fields of wheat' as a child.* Available at: https://www.independent.co.uk/news/uk/politics/theresa-may-naughtiest-thing-runnig-fields-wheat-child-tory-leader-conservatives-a7774841.html (Accessed: 24 January 2022).

Tondo, L. (2021) Football's coming to Rome? Italy fans look to Wembley showdown. Available at: https://www.theguardian.com/football/2021/jul/08/footballs-coming-to-rome-italy-fans-on-the-wembley-showdown (Accessed: 24 January 2022).

Wikipedia (n.d.) *List of most-subscribed YouTube channels.* Available at: https://en.wikipedia.org/wiki/List_of_most-subscribed_YouTube_channels (Accessed: 24 January 2022).

Knowyourmeme (n.d.) *The Great Subscriber War / Subscribe to PewDiePie*. Available at: https://knowyourmeme.com/memes/events/the-great-subscriber-war-subscribe-to-pewdiepie (Accessed: 24 January 2022).

Images

Figure 1. @TechnicallyRon (2020) *Love Actually Boris Johnson meme*. [Online image] Available at: https://thetab.com/uk/2019/12/10/boris-johnson-love-actually-video-memes-134827 (Accessed: 24 January 2022).

Figure 2. Reddit (2021) *It's Coming Home screaming meme*. [Online image] Available at: https://www.reddit.com/r/memes/comments/oatsy3/its_coming_home/ (Accessed: 24 January 2022).

Figure 3. Knowyourmeme (2019) Avengers It's Coming Home meme. [Online image] Available at: https://knowyourmeme.com/photos/1389316-its-coming-home-three-lions (Accessed: 24 January 2022).

Figure 4. me.me (n.d.) Rickrolling meme. [Online image] Available at: https://me.me/i/when-you-memorize-the-url-so-you-cant-get-rick-57c7e4b396664641bf0756de008e64b6 (Accessed: 24 January 2022).

Figure 5. @TheOxfordMail (2019) Subscribe to PewDiePie. [Online image] Available at: https://twitter.com/threader/status/1111337486909956098 (Accessed: 24 January 2022).

Figure 6. Comedy Central UK, (2017) Brexit: A Titanic Disaster. [Online image] Available at: https://www.youtube.com/watch?v=svwslRDTyzU (Accessed: 24 January 2022).

Figure 7. Comedy Central UK, (2017) Brexit: A Titanic Disaster. [Online image] Available at: https://www.youtube.com/watch?v=svwslRDTyzU (Accessed: 24 January 2022).

Figure 8. @anaveragebrit (2019) May PornHub meme. [Online image] Available at: https://www.instagram.com/p/BuD9Qqwl7fG/ (Accessed: 24 January 2022).

Figure 9. @meme.culture.lab (2020) May Corona meme. [Online image] Available at: https://www.instagram.com/p/B_FBMX2FAIH/ (Accessed: 24 January 2022).

Figure 10. @madeinpoortaste (2021) Boris drug raid. [Online image] Available at: https://www.instagram.com/p/CXLlSeJquJJ/ (Accessed: 24 January 2022).

Figure 11. @wallofcomedy (2021) Xmas Party. [Online image] Available at: https://www.instagram.com/p/CXPRrjLNwvr/ (Accessed: 24 January 2022).

Figure 12. @Fxshionconcept (2021) Squid Game snap invite. [Online image] Available at: https://www.instagram.com/p/CUsfpOjoAyP/ (Accessed: 24 January 2022).

Figure 13. @Ladbible (2021) Matt Hancock help out meme. [Online image] Available at: https://www.instagram.com/p/CQie13Do3F2/ (Accessed: 24 January 2022).

Figure 14. @lockdown.memes (2020) Boris Johnson Futurist meme. [Online image] Available at: https://www.instagram.com/p/CJtu1vMFPLM/ (Accessed: 24 January 2022).

Figure 15. @meme_0_rat (2020) Simpsons Corona meme. [Online image] Available at: https://www.instagram.com/p/B9_-hSlo_cx/ (Accessed: 24 January 2022).

Printed in Great Britain
by Amazon